"What do you v
then?" Luke asked.

"I want to stay here even if my brother and sister-in-law leave," Storm said, looking at him from under her lashes. She knew she was flirting with him.

"You'd be alone here—except for me," he said enigmatically.

She realized he was going to force her to make all the moves. "But you'd look after me, wouldn't you," she went on, "if I needed anything?"

He gave her a slow smile. "That might depend on what you need."

"Well, if I got lonely." Her heart began to beat erratically.

"In that case I think you really ought to have someone to keep you company," Luke said insinuatingly as his hands began to caress her.

"Who...do you suggest?" she asked unsteadily.

Luke's only answer was to smile knowingly into her eyes.

SALLY WENTWORTH began her publishing career at a Fleet Street newspaper in London, where she thrived in the hectic atmosphere. After her marriage, she and her husband moved to rural Hertfordshire, where Sally had been raised. Although she worked for the publisher of a group of magazines, the day soon came when her own writing claimed her energy and time. Her romance novels are often set in fascinating foreign locales.

Books by Sally Wentworth

HARLEQUIN PRESENTS

HARLEQUIN ROMANCE

Don't miss any of our special offers. Write to us at the following address for information on our newest releases.

Harlequin Reader Service
901 Fuhrmann Blvd., P.O. Box 1397, Buffalo, NY 14240
Canadian address: P.O. Box 603,
Fort Erie, Ont. L2A 5X3

SALLY WENTWORTH

satan's island

Harlequin Books

TORONTO • NEW YORK • LONDON
AMSTERDAM • PARIS • SYDNEY • HAMBURG
STOCKHOLM • ATHENS • TOKYO • MILAN

Harlequin Presents first edition April 1989
ISBN 0-373-11165-7

Original hardcover edition published in 1988
by Mills & Boon Limited

CHAPTER ONE

'MISS SHELLEY?'

Storm slowly lifted angry blue eyes and let them travel up the length of the man standing in front of her. He was dressed in old, faded denims and a bush shirt, and was so tall that Storm almost had a crick in her neck by the time she reached his tanned, angular face. 'Yes,' she acknowledged with a cold nod.

'My name's Luke Ballinger. Jerry couldn't make it, so he asked me to pick you up and fly you over to Taruna. The plane's waiting on the tarmac, if you're ready to go.'

'I have been *ready to go* for nearly four hours,' Storm informed him icily. She got up from the uncomfortable airport chair and, as she was tall herself, this brought her nearer the man's level, but she still had to tilt her head to look at him. 'Why couldn't my brother come to meet me?'

Luke Ballinger lifted one angled eyebrow at her tone but merely shrugged. 'I guess he had something else to do.'

His casual attitude, as if she was of little importance, made Storm even angrier; she was used to people jumping to help her, especially men, willing to do almost anything to receive a smile or a word of thanks from someone so famous. But this man, a mere second-rate pilot, seemed as if he couldn't care less.

5

'Just what time did Jerry arrange for you to be here?' she demanded suspiciously, certain that Jerry and his wife, Anne, would never have left her alone in a foreign airport for so long.

'Oh, he told me what time you were due here, if that's what you're getting at, but I had some business in town that took . . .'

'So it's *your* fault!' Storm snapped, the fragile hold on her temper breaking. 'Do you realise that my plane got in from Hong Kong at ten-thirty this morning? I've been stuck in this hell-hole they erroneously call an airport ever since. There's nowhere you can leave your luggage, and even if there was I doubt if it would be safe. There's no air-conditioning, nowhere to get a drink or something to eat. I've just had to sit here and watch my luggage like a hawk for *four* hours,' her voice rose in fury, 'until you, a—a mere hired pilot, decide that you're ready to come and get me!'

There were plenty of people standing around in the airport building, none of whom seemed to have anything much to do, and they gathered round interestedly as Storm let fly at the pilot. He drew himself up, his hands on his hips and his jaw hardening. 'Finished?' he asked tersely.

'No, I haven't,' Storm retorted angrily. 'I shall speak to my brother about you the moment we get to Taruna.'

'You do that,' he agreed, his mouth twisting into a thin, cynical smile. 'I'm sure he'll be pleased to hear what you have to say.'

Storm glanced at him, wondering what he meant, but he was looking at her luggage. The seven matching suitcases of various sizes, all in blue leather and with her initials on them, were stacked beside her, her cased guitar on the top, but her jewel case she held tightly in her hand. For most of the time she'd been waiting she had been the only European in the airport, and she didn't feel at all safe.

Luke Ballinger's eyebrows rose. 'Is this all yours?'

'Yes, of course. You'll have to find a porter to take it out to the plane.'

He gave a short impatient laugh. 'One case would have done for where you're going.' But he spoke to a couple of the men hovering nearby in a language that Storm didn't recognise and they each picked up two cases. Luke picked up the heaviest two and Storm followed with her jewel case, her handbag and the guitar. 'Wait! What about the other case? You'll have to get another man to carry it.'

But Luke Ballinger was already striding towards the door leading to the tarmac. Storm looked round at the crowd of natives still gathered around her, many of them grinning widely, and to Storm's mind villainously, and she hastily hung the guitar on her back, grabbed up the case and with difficulty carried it after the pilot's tall figure.

The plane was waiting on the edge of the single runway, a small two-seater that looked very fragile after the big jets that Storm was used to. Looking at it, she began to wonder just why she had arranged to make this trip.

Luke was heaving her cases into the back of the plane and turned to watch as she came struggling up. He didn't come forward to help at all, just stood there with that sardonic smile on his lips as she almost dragged the case across.

'Thanks for your help,' she said in angry sarcasm.

But sarcasm where this man was concerned was a

waste of time, he only grinned more widely and easily lifted the case into the plane with the others. 'Be careful of that guitar,' Storm ordered. 'It's extremely valuable.'

'Sure.' He picked it up and tossed it casually into the back. 'Anything else?'

She glared at him, wishing now that she'd let her manager accompany her at least this far. Wayne would have known how to shield her from a man like this; he would never have allowed anyone to speak to her in that brusque, almost rude manner, let alone make her carry her own cases. But she had decided that she needed a break from Wayne as well as from work and had insisted on him and her dresser taking a holiday too, leaving them to go straight back to England from Hong Kong.

But it was too late to regret that now, and the pilot was waiting for her to climb into the plane. Storm was wearing a white suit with a straight skirt and short-sleeved jacket that had seemed perfect when she set out from Hong Kong. Now she wasn't so sure. 'Aren't there any steps?' she asked, looking round.

'Sure. You put your foot on to this step here,' he told her, pointing to a small cavity in the side of the plane, 'and then you step on to the wing.'

'I meant, aren't there any proper boarding steps?' Storm explained.

'Look, this isn't Heathrow or JFK. There are only two scheduled flights into this airport in a week, and then it's only a stop on the way to New Guinea. They don't go in for the niceties here. If you want to get in the plane you have to get yourself in.'

She gave him a fulminating look but said, 'Hold this,' as she handed him her jewel case. Hitching up her skirt, she revealed a pair of long, shapely legs in high-heeled sandals to the interested gaze of the pilot as well as the two natives who had carried her cases and were still standing around. Putting her foot into the step, Storm pulled herself up, but it was difficult in high heels and she wobbled as she went to step on to the wing. Immediately a large hand was placed on her behind and she was almost thrown into the plane.

'Well, really! Of all the nerve!' Storm turned to glare at Luke Ballinger as he climbed in beside her, her dignity in shreds.

'Lady, it was either that or fall on to the tarmac. Now will you just strap up and shut up while I get this plane into the air?'

Storm would have liked to have said a whole lot of things, but she was beginning to wonder about his abilities as a pilot and decided it might be better not to distract him. Putting on the headset, he had a brief word with the lonely control tower that Storm could see out on the edge of the field, then they taxied on to the single runway and took off smoothly into the air. During the course of her career Storm had flown hundreds of times to all parts of the world, and it came as naturally as being driven in a car, but only on a few occasions had she travelled in small planes, and those usually private jets. She couldn't remember having flown in one as small as this since she and Jerry had gone up in a plane for the very first time, at an air show when they were children. Jerry, she remembered, had resolved there and then that he would learn to fly, an ambition he had eventually achieved some fifteen years later, but it was only as a sideline, an added advantage to his career as a civil engineer.

Storm had loved the flight too, looking down over England's green, rolling pasture-land. But here it was all so different. Once they had left the airport behind the town around it soon gave way to a few miles of cultivated paddy fields which soon merged into the deeper green of the forest. But this stopped abruptly at the long golden curve of the coastline, and then they were over the open sea, heading for Taruna, the island where Jerry was working as a site director for a civil engineering company who were building a dam and power station.

'Do we have far to go?' she asked when Luke took off the headset and put the plane on automatic pilot.

'It should take us about three hours with this wind.' Reaching into a locker beside his seat, he took out a flask. 'Coffee?'

'*Please!* I'm so thirsty. I had an extremely long wait,' she added tartly, remembering.

Luke didn't rise to the jibe, just handing her the lid of the flask half filled with thick black coffee.

'Is there any milk and sugar?' He just raised an eloquent eyebrow at her, so Storm had to drink it as it came. It was bitter and set her teeth on edge, but hot and thirst-quenching, making her feel better as soon as she drank it. Taking a tissue from her bag, she carefully wiped the cup before handing it back to Luke. 'Thank you,' she said stiffly.

He nodded, apparently a man of few words, his grey eyes covering the horizon in a casual way that Storm somehow thought was deceptive. It was lucky that she was thin, because Luke was definitely too tall and too broad for the little plane, taking up most of the room in the cabin. As it was their shoulders touched and several times his bare arm brushed hers as he moved to reach the controls.

Storm felt hot and sticky and longed for a cold shower. The dull headache that she seemed to get more and more often nowadays had turned into a nagging pain. She was so looking foward to this holiday, to having a complete break from work and fans and television, away from everyone and everything to do with her career. At first, after she had gone to see a doctor and he had advised her to rest, she had told Wayne that she wanted a holiday and he had suggested hiring a house in the West Indies or in the South of France, with only him and her dresser and secretary for company—as well as servants to look after them, of course. The other members of the growing retinue of people that seemed essential whenever she went on tour or made an appearance would be left behind. She had almost agreed, but he had mentioned getting her music arranger over and working out some songs for a new album, and she had realised that it wouldn't be the break she so desperately needed. Then she had thought of Jerry and Anne, who had been living on Taruna in the South Pacific for the past year. On a tiny island like that no one would know her and she would be able to get a complete rest. So when her current tour ended in Hong Kong she had travelled on alone—the first time she had ever been really alone in years. She had had to argue quite a lot to get her own way, and for some reason that she didn't know herself she had lied to Wayne, giving him a false address so that he couldn't contact her.

Storm sat back in her seat and tried to relax, putting

up a hand with long, painted fingernails to remove the big, square sunglasses she habitually wore. Closing her eyes, she rubbed the bridge of her nose with her thumb and forefinger to try to relieve the headache, opening them again when she felt the pilot move beside her. He was watching her, a slight frown between his eyes. 'You OK?' She nodded, but he added, 'You're sure not going to be sick or anything?'

A smile lit her eyes, eyes that were a clear Wedgwood blue and were her most famous feature after her hair. 'You don't have to worry—I've never been ill on a plane yet.'

'You don't look too good,' Luke said bluntly, in no way reassured. 'If you *are* going to be sick for God's sake use the bag. Or else, I warn you, you clear it up yourself.'

'You've got a nerve!' Storm snapped in annoyance. 'Are you as rude as this to all your passengers?'

'I don't get many like you.' He didn't add 'thank God', but the words were implicit in his tone.

'I'm surprised you get any at all,' Storm retorted. 'Do you own this plane or does it belong to a charter company?'

Luke altered course after glancing at the map strapped to his thigh, then turned to look at her, his grey eyes running over her mockingly. 'Neither. It belongs to the L.B. Group.'

'Who are they?'

'That's the company your brother works for.'

So Luke Ballinger must be the company pilot. Storm was hardly surprised that that was the only job he could get if he was always this surly. But at least he seemed a capable enough pilot.

'Where are we?' she asked him, looking down into the still green sea with here and there on the horizon the outlines of small islands, some thick with vegetation, some flat and bare.

'We're flying over the Molucca Passage.'

'Not the Pacific?'

'No, the ocean is farther north.'

'There seem to be a lot of islands down there,' she observed.

'There are—dozens of them.'

Storm just hoped he knew which one they were heading for, but then dismissed it from her mind. There was nothing she could do about it either way, so she leaned back again, feeling terribly tired. Her hair was pinned into a neat coil at the back of her head, but this felt uncomfortable against the headrest, so she lifted a lazy hand and pulled out the pins, letting the heavy red-gold tresses tumble loosely about her shoulders. Her eyelids began to close, but she suddenly remembered her jewel case lying at her feet. The case was locked, but she had an idea that Luke Ballinger might be an expert with a screwdriver, so she picked up the case and held it tightly in her hands before closing her eyes again.

Within two minutes she was asleep, lulled by the steady drone of the plane's engine as it travelled on across the empty skies, unaware of Luke's scrutiny as he took a rest and turned to look his fill at her sleeping form, his mouth twisting wryly as he saw the way she was clutching her jewel case.

It was about an hour later that Storm awoke and found that she had turned in her sleep, her head now resting on the pilot's shoulder. She blinked and sat up, pushing her hair off her face.

'You must have been really tired,' he commented.

'Yes, I was. Er—sorry.'

Luke shrugged. 'It's OK.'

He altered course so that the sun came into the cockpit. It was lower in the sky now, and Storm glanced at her watch. Six o'clock—they must be almost there. She peered out of the windscreen, looking for signs of Taruna, but the sea was empty.

'It will be another twenty minutes before we see it,' Luke informed her.

'Is it a big island?'

'About half the size of Scotland.'

'Does much go on there?'

'Depends what you mean.'

Storm gave him an irritated glance, thinking he was being purposely dense. 'I mean are there many tourists there? Lots of hotels and country clubs, that sort of thing?'

Luke gave a laugh of surprised amusement. 'No, there aren't. In fact there are very few Europeans there at all.'

Storm gave an inner sigh of relief and satisfaction; this was exactly what she wanted, to get right away from so-called civilisation for a while. But Luke, of course, took it the wrong way. 'If you expected that kind of holiday, you're in for a big surprise,' he said brusquely. 'Taruna isn't a tourist resort. There aren't any luxury hotels or night clubs. If that's what you want you might just as well turn round and go back!' he added disparagingly.

'I came to see my brother and sister-in-law,' Storm pointed out shortly.

'How long do you intend staying?'

'Two or three weeks, perhaps longer. It depends.'

Again Luke gave that derisive laugh. 'I'll give you two days. After that you'll be bored as hell and want to go home. Back to your nightclubs and all the other luxuries you won't be able to live without.'

'You're mistaken,' Storm corrected him shortly. 'I'm quite capable of living a simple life.'

He turned to look at her, his eyes running over her carefully made-up face, the white silk suit and expensive sandals. He looked at her heavy gold necklace, at the rings and bracelets on her hands, and those long, painted fingernails. 'I was wrong,' he said sardonically. 'I'll only give you one day before you start missing your jacuzzi, your limo and your hairdresser. Before you start wanting to call up your friends and go to cocktail parties. Before you get bored to death with only Jerry and Anne to fawn over you instead of all those hordes of fans who all think you're so glamorous and wonderful.'

So he did at least know who she was; Storm had begun to doubt it. Angry spots of colour rose in her cheeks. The insufferable man! No one had dared to speak to her like that in years. Glaring at him, she said, 'For a two-bit pilot you really think you know everything, don't you? No wonder this was the only job you could get! I'm only surprised that you manage to keep it. Tell me,' she added contemptuously, 'is it because *you're* such a failure that you're jealous of people who are successful?'

Immediately she had said it she felt ashamed; after all, how was she to know what had brought him this low? But her remarks didn't annoy him at all. He merely gave her a derisive look and strapped himself into his seat again. 'Hold on to your jewel case, lady, we're going in to land.'

Storm hadn't even realised that Taruna had come into sight, but there it was, getting rapidly larger on the horizon. A lush green island of forest and palm trees, rising to craggy mountains in the centre, and along its coastline the golden sweep of long sandy beaches, still lagoons, and the white caps of waves breaking over the reefs that guarded the island like an undersea wall.

There was only one town of any size, she could see it over on her left, but Luke flew on into the centre of the island, over the forest towards the mountains. He flew lower, between the hills, and the plane began to be buffeted a little by the thermals of air rising from the ground. Storm put out a hand to steady herself, but she wasn't afraid, in fact she was rather enjoying it. A big clearing came into sight and Luke circled over it, positioning the plane to land on the roughly cut airstrip. Below her she could see where the dam was well on its way to being constructed, men like worker ants swarming all over the site and with a lot of plant and buildings, workers' accommodation presumably, alongside it. Further off, on the side of the hill, there were two bungalows shaded by trees, their tiny gardens alive with tropical flowers, which was where she guessed Jerry must live. But before she could see anything else, Luke was bringing the plane down on to the grass runway.

He taxied over to a hangar, and as soon as the plane stopped Jerry pulled open the door. Storm gave a cry of pleasure and hastily undid her straps to almost fall into his arms. They hugged each other enthusiastically and both began to talk at once, then burst into laughter and hugged each other all over again.

'Marvellous! Marvellous to see you,' Jerry exclaimed. He held her at arm's length to look at her. 'You look great. Beautiful! Who'd have thought that my little sister would grow up to be so talented and famous?'

Storm pulled a face at him. She hadn't seen him for nearly two years and as Jerry was the only member of her family she had left—their parents having died some time ago—this felt almost like coming home. 'How's Anne?' she asked. 'Congratulations on the baby, by the way. Do you want a boy or a girl?'

Jerry laughed and put his arm round her shoulders. 'I want a girl and Anne wants a boy, so I've told her she'll just have to have twins!' He broke off as he saw Luke getting the cases out of the plane and went over to him. 'Here, let me do that. Good grief, is this luggage all yours, Storm?'

They pulled the cases out, together with a navy holdall.

'That doesn't belong to me,' Storm pointed out.

'No, that's mine.' Luke pulled a jacket out of the back and picked up the holdall.

'Thanks very much for picking Storm up, Luke. It was very good of you. I'm extremely grateful.'

Luke gave a brief nod, an amused glint in his eyes as he saw the look of indignant surprise on Storm's face at Jerry's appreciative, almost deferential tone. He walked away, heading towards the bungalows on the hill.

Jerry beckoned up some men to carry her luggage, then put his arm round Storm's shoulders again as they followed Luke up the track. 'It's wonderful to have you here,' he told her. 'Anne has so been looking forward to having some female company.'

'Aren't there any other women here?' Storm enquired.

'There are two who are half Dutch, half Malay, but apart from that there are only native women at the site. Anne has tried to make friends, but the language is a problem, and the backgrounds are so different that it's difficult to bridge the gap. There are some European women in Bura, of course—that's the main town on the other side of the island—and we go over there a couple of times a month. But I know that she gets lonely, so having you here will be a wonderful tonic for her.'

'How's she coping with being pregnant out here?'

Jerry's mouth twisted wryly. 'Not too well, I'm afraid. I take her in to see the doctor in Bura regularly, and she tries not to complain, but she's very low.'

'I'll have to do my best to cheer her up, then.' Storm glanced ahead of them towards the bungalows and saw Luke stepping through the door of the one on the right. 'Does he live in that house?' she asked.

Jerry followed her gaze. 'Luke? He's using it while he's here. He doesn't come to the site all that often. But we've had some trouble w——' He broke off as a woman appeared at the door of the left-hand house and began to run down the path to meet them. 'Here's Anne.'

Storm hurried forward to meet her sister-in-law and the two embraced affectionately.

'Darling, congratulations on the baby. I'm so looking forward to being a doting aunt. How are you? You're so tanned!'

'Oh, I'm fine,' said Anne. 'Come into the house. You must be tired out after that long journey.'

But for all she'd said that she was fine, Storm had to agree with her brother that Anne was looking thin and far from well. But her eyes, now, were alight with excitement as she ushered Storm into the house and fussed over her, offering her a cold drink and some home-made biscuits, and making her sit down and rest. Jerry joined them after he'd taken Storm's cases into her room and for half an hour or so they sat and chatted, catching up on all the news. But they had few friends in common now, both of them having moved away from their home town several years ago, so Storm asked Jerry about his work on the dam. 'Will you be here much longer?'

'About another three months, if all goes well.' Jerry frowned, looking worried. 'But there's been quite a lot of political unrest on the island lately. We've had to bring skilled workers in from Borneo and Celebes and they don't get on with the natives of Taruna. That's why I wasn't able to come and meet you myself today: I had to stay here and sort out a spot of bother. But luckily Luke was due to fly in, so I radioed and asked him to bring you instead.'

'I wanted to have a word with you about him,' Storm said feelingly, remembering the pilot's rudeness. 'He may be a good pilot, but as far as public relations go, he's absolutely hopeless!'

'Public relations? What on earth do you mean?' asked Anne, puzzled.

'Well, to put it bluntly, he was darn rude. For a start he kept me waiting for over four hours and didn't even have the grace to apologise. And then he made me carry one of my cases and wouldn't help me into the cockpit.' Her eyes flashed as she remembered the way she'd been shoved aboard. 'Well, at least he did, but in the most ill-mannered way. I told him what I thought of him, but I really think *you* should give him a ticking off, Jerry. After all, he's only the company pilot, and if he treated *me* that way how would he behave towards anyone important who came to the site? I really . . .' Storm's voice faded as she saw that both Jerry and Anne were listening to her with looks of fascinated horror on their faces. 'What is it? Why are you looking at me like that?'

'Luke isn't the company pilot!' Anne exclaimed.

'Who is he, then?'

'He just happens to be my boss,' Jerry said on a groan. 'And not only my boss, but the head of the company that's building the dam and the power station.'

'I don't believe it!' gasped Storm. 'He can't possibly be! Why, he was only wearing quite old clothes and he . . .' Her voice failed as she looked at their faces. 'He's really the head of the whole set-up?'

'The construction company is called the L.B. Group. L.B. stands for Luke Ballinger,' Jerry said hollowly. 'He not only heads the company, he built it up and takes a meticulous interest in every aspect of it. That's why he's here; he knew that we were getting behind schedule and came to find out why for himself.'

'Were you *very* rude to him?' asked Anne.

'No more than he was to me. Anyway, he asked for it. He was damned arrogant—at least I thought he was, for a pilot.' Storm pulled a comical face. 'I suppose as the big boss he thought he had a right to be.'

Anne suddenly burst out laughing. 'I wish I'd been there to see you tell him off! I don't think anyone's dared to say a word against Luke in years!'

Jerry tried to frown but couldn't keep his face straight and he, too, joined in their laughter. And of course, it just had to be at that moment that the houseboy opened the door and Luke strode into the room.

Jerry stopped laughing so abruptly that he began to choke, and Anne turned bright red, so leaving Luke in no doubt whatsoever that they had been laughing at him.

He gave Storm a sardonic look. 'Brightening the place up already, I see.'

Refusing to be intimidated, she gave him a cool nod. 'It was a funny story.'

'I can imagine.'

'I thought you might.' Her eyes met Luke's challengingly. So he was rich and successful instead of being just a pilot. So what? Just because he had power it didn't give him the right to be rude and arrogant. You could have good manners whatever kind of job you did. Even though she was rich and famous herself, Storm always made a point of trying to be polite and pleasant to everyone she came in contact with.

Turning to Jerry, Luke said, 'I'm sorry to interrupt your reunion, but I wonder if you could spare me half an hour or so? I learnt one or two things on the way here that I think you ought to know about.'

'Yes, of course.' Jerry got immediately to his feet.

'Let's take a walk.' Luke opened the door but paused to smile at Anne. It was only a social smile, but it made him look quite different, younger and more approachable. 'Don't worry, Anne, I promise he'll be back in time for dinner.'

'Oh, that's all right. It won't be for nearly an hour yet.' She hesitated. 'Perhaps you'd like to join us?'

'Thanks, but I don't want to intrude on you tonight—and I do have several things that I'd like to get out of the way so that I'll have tomorrow free to concentrate on the site.'

'Oh, well, if you're staying over why don't you come to dinner tomorrow evening instead?'

'I'd like that very much. Thank you.' Luke gave Anne a nod of thanks, but as he turned away to follow Jerry through the door Storm saw that he had a thin smile of amusement on his lips that she instinctively knew was because he'd guessed that she didn't want him there.

When the men had gone Storm gave a moue of distaste and said, 'I suppose you had no choice but to invite him. If you're the only European woman on the site he must expect you to offer him hospitality every time he comes here. You're lucky he doesn't want to stay with you instead of in the other bungalow.'

'Oh, no, he wouldn't do that,' Anne said positively. 'He has a native girl who looks after him whenever he comes to stay.' Storm gave her a quick look, wondering just how well the girl looked after Luke, but Anne's face was completely innocent as she went on to say, 'You mustn't think we don't like Luke. We do. He's been very kind to us—especially to me. He realises that I get a bit lonely and does his best to help. And he's made such a fuss of me ever since Jerry told him about the baby. Every time a plane comes in with supplies, there's always a basket of fresh fruit and a parcel of foodstuffs for me.' She laughed. 'He says I need building up, but how he expects caviar and preserves to be good for a baby, I don't know! He obviously hasn't much experience on the subject.'

'He isn't married, then,' Storm commented. 'I'm hardly surprised. No woman in her right mind would want to be tied to him.'

Anne smiled. 'You've obviously got off on the wrong foot with Luke. He's really very kind.'

Storm didn't believe her, but she let it pass. 'When is the baby due?' she asked.

A soft look came into Anne's face as she put a hand over her stomach. 'In about five months. Does it show yet? I wondered whether I ought to start thinking about maternity clothes.'

As, apart from a slight thickening around her waist, Anne looked thinner than she normally did, Storm had to make a tactful reply. 'It doesn't show much yet. I expect it will all happen suddenly. You'll have to get Jerry to take you to Hong Kong for a weekend—you can get beautiful clothes there.'

'That would be nice,' Anne said wistfully. 'But I don't know if Jerry could get the time off. He's working flat out, you see, to try to get the dam finished on schedule. If he does, that will give us a couple of months before the baby's due to arrive and he'll be able to come back to England with me. He'll be so worried if I have to go back alone.'

'Isn't there a hospital in Bura? Can't you have the baby there?'

Anne's face shadowed. 'I could, I suppose, but I'd much rather go home so that my mother can look after me afterwards.'

'Can't she come out here, if it's necessary?'

'Oh no, she'd hate it here. And anyway, she's afraid of flying.'

Storm thought that a pretty poor excuse, but only having met Anne's mother once, at their wedding, she was in no position to really have an opinion on whether she was just being selfish. 'If you like,' she offered, 'I'll arrange for a nurse to come and look after you. I'd come myself, but I don't know a thing about babies, and somehow I don't think you'd have much confidence in me.'

'That's very kind of you.' Anne smiled at her warmly. 'Maybe we will take you up on the offer of the nurse, if the need arises, but as I said, we hope to be back in England by then.' She laughed. 'And you're quite right, I just can't imagine you trying to cope with a baby—you're far too glamorous!' A shadow flickered across Storm's eyes at that, but Anne didn't see it. 'And besides,' she added, 'you have your career to think of. You could hardly disappoint your fans by cancelling engagements just to come and look after me!'

'I would if you needed me,' Storm replied calmly.

Anne shook her head, not believing her. 'I was just so surprised when you wrote to say you were coming this time.'

'I felt like a holiday.'

'And I expect you feel like a shower after that journey.' Anne got to her feet. 'I'll show you your room, shall I?'

Storm followed her down a corridor with several doors opening off it to a room on the far right. It was a pleasant room with French doors opening on to the veranda that went all round the building and with a window set in the other wall that looked across to the neighbouring bungalow. The room was adequately furnished and had a quite large bed with a mosquito net ready to be draped over it.

'A mosquito net! Good heavens, I've never slept under one of those before!' Storm exclaimed.

'I hope you'll be comfortable,' Anne said rather anxiously. 'It's so different from what you're used to.'

Putting her hand on Anne's arm, Storm gave it a little shake. 'Hey, this is me, remember? Jerry's sister.'

'Yes, of course,' Anne agreed—but added, 'But you're so famous now. And so—successful.' By which she meant rich. 'Your standards must have changed completely. Life must be very different for you from when you were at home.'

'Life may be different, but *I'm* not,' Storm assured her.

Anne nodded. 'Of course—sorry. Would you like me to unpack for you?'

'Certainly not, but I'd better have that shower or I'll be late for dinner.'

As Storm began to unpack as much as the wardrobe and chest of drawers in the room would hold, she pondered on what Anne had said. Had her standards really changed so much? Certainly this room seemed very small when she compared it to the hotel suites she usually stayed in and the bedroom of her own flat in London, but it was much bigger than the room she'd had at home before her parents died. All things were relative, she supposed. You grew to expand into the space around you.

Before she changed, Storm went over to the windows to close the shutters, and saw Jerry and Luke standing together farther up the hill. They were talking earnestly, or at least Luke was talking while Jerry listened attentively. They were both tall men, but Jerry was thin and wiry, his fair hair already beginning to recede a little, whereas Luke was very powerfully built, his chest and shoulders wide and strong, his legs as solid as tree-trunks, and his hair still thick and dark. As she watched them, Luke made a gesture towards the site, glancing up as he did so and catching sight of her at the window. He must have paused in what he was saying, because Jerry started to turn round, but Storm quickly closed the shutters and fastened them with a brass catch.

The bungalow had both electricity and running water laid on, amenities that Storm had taken for granted would be here before she arrived, but which she now realised were luxuries in a place like this. She made full use of them, taking a long shower and then drying her hair with the blowdrier. When she peeped through the slats in the shutters she saw that the two men had gone, and presently she heard Jerry's voice in the sitting-room.

They had a pleasant meal, just the three of them, but Storm found that even Jerry was a little in awe of her success, but both he and Anne were pleased with the numerous presents she'd brought for them. 'I'm overwhelmed!' Jerry exclaimed, looking at the expensive set of men's toiletries that he'd just opened. 'You really shouldn't have, Storm.'

'Nonsense! You two are all I've got. Who else can I buy presents for, for heaven's sake?'

'All right, all right,' Jerry laughed. 'The workmen are going to give me some funny looks if I turn up on site with this aftershave on!'

They talked for an hour or so longer and Storm sipped at a long, iced drink, but she suddenly felt terribly tired again. It was something that had been happening to her more frequently during the last few weeks and one of the main reasons why she had seen a doctor and decided to take a holiday. It wasn't just the normal tiredness one feels after a long journey or from working too hard, but a sudden feeling that all her strength and energy had drained from her.

Interrupting Jerry in the middle of a sentence, she said, 'I'm so sorry, but I can't keep my eyes open any longer. Will you excuse me?'

She fell asleep almost at once, but there was no air-conditioning, which she'd got used to in her luxury hotel in Hong Kong, and she slept only restlessly. She dreamt that she was being stifled by cobwebs which kept floating down on top of her, layer after layer, until she could hardly breathe, and all the time Luke Ballinger was standing by laughing. With a cry Storm awoke and sat up, pushing the cobwebs violently away, only to find that a corner of the mosquito net had come loose and lay across her. Her face was wet with perspiration and the room hot and stuffy.

Getting out of bed, she washed her face, her hands trembling. God, how she hated waking up like this from a nightmare, but at least this one had a cause and was different from the terrible recurring dream she usually suffered from. She pushed the shutters open; she just had to have air whether the mosquitoes got in or not. It was still relatively early, the moon was out and she could hear distant noises coming from the site where some men were actually still working. Did Luke drive his men that hard, then? Storm glanced across at the neighbouring bungalow and saw that a light was burning in one of the rooms. As she watched she saw

Luke's silhouette come near to the window, and then
that of a woman, who came up and stood very close to
him. The native girl who looked after the house,
presumably. The two talked for a few moments, Luke's
figure a good head and shoulders taller than that of the
girl. Then they moved away from the window
together—and the light went out. Storm stepped back,
feeling slightly unclean, like a voyeur. So Luke Ballinger
was having an affair with the girl! Well, it was no more
than she'd expected of him. But even so she felt a shiver
of revulsion as she re-closed the shutters and went back
to bed.

CHAPTER TWO

THE following day Jerry was busy with Luke on the site, so Anne and Storm went for a short walk, neither of them feeling very energetic, and spent the rest of the morning sunbathing in the garden at the back of the house where they couldn't be overlooked. Anne had a fascinated interest in Storm's career and wanted to know about all the famous people she had met and the places where she had appeared. Storm did her best to oblige, but she hadn't slept after the nightmare and she was soon dozing in the sun, her eyelids just too heavy to stay open any longer.

Jerry came home at lunchtime, but he just ate quickly and left again, his mind obviously preoccupied and a continuous frown of worry between his eyes.

'Is the dam very much behind schedule?' Storm asked Anne when he had gone.

'Only a couple of weeks, which really isn't very much on a big project like this. And that's only because some of the materials they need haven't been getting through on time. It isn't Jerry's fault—there's been some trouble at the dock at Bura.'

'What kind of trouble?'

'I'm not really sure. Just some political disturbances, Jerry said.'

Storm gave her a reflective look, wondering if Jerry

was playing things down so that Anne wouldn't
worry. He certainly seemed over-anxious for a mere
delay of materials. Resolving to question her brother
more fully when they were alone, she changed the
subject by asking Anne if she could help with the
preparations for dinner.

'Oh no, it's nearly all taken care of. Our houseboy
does most of the cooking, although he does tend to
make things much too spicy for European palates, but
I suppose we've got used to it by now.'

Storm gave her a direct look. 'Have you been very
ill during this pregnancy, Anne?' she asked.

The older girl flushed. 'Has Jerry been talking to
you?' A thought came to her and her head came up.
'Did he send for you? Is that why you've come here so
suddenly?'

'Good heavens, no!' Storm's answer was too
surprised to be anything but sincere. 'Why on earth
would Jerry send for *me*? He knows I'm hopeless
where sick people are concerned. Hasn't he told you?
I hate hospitals and illness so much that I wouldn't
even visit him when he was ill in hospital that time
before you were married. I don't think he's ever
forgiven me for it,' she added lightly. 'No, I came here
because I wanted a rest. I can't remember the last time
I had a real holiday. And as my tour ended in Hong
Kong it seemed an ideal opportunity to come and
spend my holiday with you.'

'Well, I'm glad you did. It's lovely to have someone
to talk to.'

Storm looked at her for a moment, wondering
whether to push it, but it was early days yet; if Anne
wanted to confide in her then she must choose her

own time.

'We'll be just the four of us for dinner,' Anne was saying. 'But I hope you don't mind, there are several company officials working here who live in a building near the site and—well, they've coerced Jerry into letting them come round to meet you after dinner. You don't mind, do you?' she repeated anxiously. 'They'd have wanted to meet you whoever you were, not just because you're such a well-known singer.'

Inwardly Storm was very annoyed; having to spend the evening in Luke Ballinger's company was bad enough, but to have to be sociable to a whole herd of men who probably hadn't been near a woman in months definitely didn't appeal, and it was far from the complete rest she'd envisaged. But she had to smile and say, 'You must invite who you like—but don't be annoyed with me if it all gets a bit much and I disappear half-way through the evening.'

The men who were coming that evening would, Storm was sure, expect to see her as she always appeared on television, wearing a slinky, glamorous dress that showed her figure off to its best advantage, heavily made-up, and with her beautiful hair in soft curls on her shoulders. Storm had a great many dresses like that, used during her last tour, but dressing up as if for a public appearance was the last thing she wanted to do here on Taruna. But then again she didn't want to let Anne and Jerry down; so she compromised by putting on a red evening dress that was cut quite low on its sequinned bodice but had long, flimsy sleeves and a full skirt. She put on quite a lot of make-up, accentuating the clear sky-blue of her eyes and the fine angles of her face, and did her hair as she wore it on stage. As always before a public appearance, she looked herself over critically in front of the mirror, frowned and hesitated a moment, then put on a diamond pendant necklace and added the big rose-cut diamond solitaire ring that had been a present from a very rich entrepreneur whose chain of theatres she had given concerts in.

'Wow!' Jerry looked at her in pleased admiration when she went into the sitting-room. 'You're going to stun them all!'

Storm pulled a face at him and went to help Anne, who was laying the table. 'Is there anything I can do?'

'Well, if you wouldn't mind bringing the flower arrangements for the table in from the kitchen.'

Storm went to do as she was asked and so missed Luke's arrival. She carried the bowls of floating frangipani blossoms into the dining-room and paused there, listening to his voice as he greeted Anne and Jerry. She still couldn't get used to the idea of him being the head of such a large company; she would have been much happier if he really had been a two-bit pilot, so that she could completely ignore him. And having an affair with a local girl didn't exactly enhance him in her eyes either. Going to the door of the sitting-room, Storm put a hand on the door jamb, waiting until there was a pause in the conversation before she went in.

Luke was listening to something Anne had started to say, but he must have caught a movement in the doorway, because he glanced up, and then his eyes widened and stayed on Storm, an arrested expression in their depths. She had seen that look in men's eyes before and her chin came up defiantly. For a moment

Luke's eyes lit with amusement, but then his face became frankly lascivious as his eyes moved down her body, mentally stripping her naked.

Her eyes flaming in suppressed anger, Storm stepped into the room and said, 'Could I have a drink, Jerry?'

'Yes, of course. Er—you remember Luke?'

Storm shot Luke a glance that had made lesser men cringe. 'Oh, yes, I remember him.'

Luke laughed easily, in no way put out. 'How are you enjoying your visit?'

'I'm enjoying it very much, thank you,' she answered coldly, recalling how he'd said she'd be bored after a day.

'You must get Jerry to show you over the dam and the power station,' he said mendaciously. 'I'm sure you'll find that stimulating.'

Anne laughed. 'I'm sure she'd hate it! Look at this super box of chocolates Luke has brought me, Storm. What with this and all the presents you brought us yesterday, if feels just like Christmas!'

They sat down to dinner, Jerry and Anne at each end of the table and Luke and Storm on the sides. Unfortunately the table wasn't very wide, and they were both tall, so their knees touched almost as soon as they sat down. Storm immediately moved hers out of the way, Luke giving her a mocking look as she did so. God, the man was insufferable! Did he think she *wanted* to touch his damned knees? Deliberately she turned to Anne and asked her about the food the houseboy had brought in. Anne was too good a hostess, though, to let Storm monopolise her, and she soon brought Luke and Jerry into the conversation.

The meal was a long one but not interminably so, the food was different from anything she had ever had before and the conversation, especially when Luke was speaking, almost stimulating. He was a good conversationalist with a wealth of stories and anecdotes to draw on. He didn't pay a lot of attention to Storm, but put himself out to be charming to Anne, making her laugh and bringing a flush of happiness to her pale face. Storm watched, joining in the conversation when she felt like it, but quite content to take a back seat and let Anne be the centre of attention. Once or twice she encountered a glance from Luke as if he was slightly puzzled at her reticence; what did he expect her to do, she thought angrily: talk about nothing but herself the whole evening?

But she was rather intrigued that Luke bothered to put himself out at all, and seeing him turn on the charm after he'd been so abrasive to her was quite a revelation. After dinner they took their coffee into the sitting-room, Storm choosing an armchair where she could stretch her legs—they felt cramped after being tucked up under her chair for so long to avoid Luke's knees! They had hardly finished their first cups of coffee before there was a loud knock on the front door and the first of Jerry's colleagues arrived. They were followed by several more until the room seemed to be filled by men who shook Storm's hand too enthusiastically and found it difficult to talk to her until they'd had a couple of stiff drinks and then would hardly stop.

The party had been going on for well over an hour, the room was noisy with raised voices and was becoming full of cigarette smoke that hung in the still air even though the windows were open. Storm's head had begun to throb and she had difficulty in extricating herself from a man who told her he was the Site Maintenance Officer, and who had cornered her to tell her his life story, which he seemed to think she would find rivetingly interesting. So far he had only got to his student days, and Storm just couldn't take any more. He had his arm stretched out in front of her as he leaned against the wall and no amount of hints would make him move. So she just ducked under his arm and headed for the door.

'Hey, Storm, when are you going to sing for us?' Another man stepped in front of her and caught her arm. In his other hand he was holding a drink and a fat acrid-smelling cigar.

She shook her head, but now most of the men in the room were crowding round her, demanding that she sing for them.

'Sorry, I'm on holiday.' She tried to push through them, but they thought she was being modest and kept up the clamour.

Not for the first time, Storm wondered why people thought that if they shouted loudly enough she would have to do as they wanted.

Again she shook her head. 'No. Sorry.' And she looked around for Jerry to come and rescue her.

But Jerry too had had a few drinks and was enjoying the reflected glory of being her brother and host to such a famous celebrity. 'Oh, come on, Storm,' he cajoled. 'Just sing one song. We won't mind about you not having an orchestra or anything to back you.'

'I could play the piano for you if you like?' Anne

offered from the side of the room where she was
standing near Luke. 'I'm not very good, but if all you
need is some music . . .'

Storm looked at them; her head felt as if knives were
being thrust into it, and the smoke was so thick it was
hurting her eyes. Their faces were all turned to her
eagerly, greedily, just as in her terrible nightmare
when all the thousands of people in the audience
became just heads with gaping mouths, like cuckoos,
wanting to suck her dry, to devour her. 'No!' she
answered on a curt, angry note. 'Don't you listen? I
am *not* going to sing!' And she pushed through them
as their faces turned from surprise to disgruntled
annoyance.

The air outside was like a balm. Storm coughed a
little and took great gasps of it into her lungs. Lord,
how she hated small, stuffy parties like that! If Wayne
had been there he would have been on the watch to
guard her from men who tried to monopolise her and
ready to whisk her away from the party as soon as she
gave him a sign. Wayne would always be at her side,
always reliable. Storm walked through the moonlit
garden to the path going up the hillside, realising just
how much she had come to rely on her manager in the
four years that he had been with her. He had taken
over not only the professional side of her life but the
private side as well, guarding her, advising, arranging
her present and her future, until all she had to worry
about was which dress to appear in and what to sing.

And then, a few weeks ago, Wayne had asked her to
marry him. It hadn't come as a complete surprise, of
course, but even so it had made Storm stop and take a
look at herself. She had been working so hard, almost

non-stop, for those four years: working in the theatre in musicals, making records, going on tour, building up her career until she was known all over the world and eagerly sought after. Right now she was supposed to be making up her mind whether to appear in a film in Hollywood or a new musical in London, and Wayne was negotiating a better deal with a new record company for another two albums.

But she was so tired, and the headaches and the nightmares were becoming more and more frequent, so that several times she had been tempted to turn to drugs to get her through a performance. So far she had managed to resist, but the doctor had told her recently that she was heading for a breakdown unless she took a complete rest. So she had come to Taruna, and she was darned if she was going to be forced into singing for a gang of building workers on only her second evening here.

She leant against the trunk of a palm tree and closed her eyes, oblivious to the soft moonlight, wishing that the men would hurry up and leave so that she could go to bed. The sound of a stone being crunched on the path made her open her eyes and she saw the tall shadow of a man walking towards her. Jerry come to find out what was the matter, she supposed. But as he came nearer she saw that the shadow was too broad. It was Luke, not Jerry.

'Anne asked me to come and find you,' he said as he reached her. 'She was worried about you.' His voice became cold and sneering. 'Although why she should worry about a spoilt brat who's just ruined her evening, I fail to see.'

Storm gave him a fulminating glance and said

scornfully, 'No, I don't suppose anyone as insensitive as you *would* understand.'

'Don't try and tell me you had some real reason not to. It wouldn't have hurt you to sing one song for them—and it would have given Anne and Jerry a lot of pleasure. But I suppose you thought it would be beneath your dignity—to sing for a bunch of uncouth men who hadn't even paid for a ticket!'

'You think I ought to have sung for my supper, is that it?' Storm retorted. But before he could answer, she went on angrily, 'And what about you? What are you going to do to earn your supper? What's *your* party trick! You're an engineer—do you think Anne and Jerry would like you to entertain everyone by showing them how to build a bridge or—or a harbour or something?'

'Don't be ridiculous!' Luke told her, his face hardening.

'What's so ridiculous about it? Why, because I happen to sing for a living, should I be expected to perform every time someone asks?'

'This is hardly just anyone. Jerry is your brother. And couldn't you have thought of those men? They've been away from their homes and families for nearly two years. They were all looking forward to meeting you, and it would have been one of the highlights of their lives to have heard you sing.'

'Then let them listen to a record,' Storm snapped back pettishly.

'You unfeeling little bitch! It's about time someone taught you that you're no better and no different from any other woman.'

'And you're just the man to do it, I suppose?' she

retorted tauntingly.

A sardonic look came into Luke's face. 'Don't tempt me, lady,' he threatened.

She laughed in his face. 'Oh, don't worry, you're the last man I'd ever want to tempt. I'm no local girl who doesn't have a choice.'

He stepped up close to her. His eyes, made menacing by a shaft of moonlight, glittered down at her. 'And just what is that supposed to mean?' he demanded dangerously.

Storm was about to make a stinging reply when she suddenly realised how close he was, and how big and—and how much of a man. Somehow this whole argument had got out of hand and come down to a personal level. She wasn't afraid of him, but now she was aware of him as a man. But that was the last thing she wanted. 'Oh, it means anything you damned well like,' she snapped at him. 'I'm going in.'

She turned to walk past him, but Luke put out a hand and caught her upper arm, his grip firm through the flimsy material of her sleeve. 'Oh, no, you don't. You started something; and you're going to finish it. What were you getting at?'

'Oh, for heaven's sake! It was just a remark, that's all. Now let go of me.'

'Not until I'm good and ready,' Luke said forcibly, his grip tightening.

Her temper flaring, Storm tried to wrench her arm away. 'You animal, take your hand off me! How *dare* you touch me?'

It was the wrong thing to say. Luke was used to being treated with deference and he too had a short cord to an explosive temper. 'Just who the hell do you

think you are?' he demanded, starting to shake her.
'I've a good mind to teach you . . .'

Storm opened her mouth and screamed. She had a
trained voice and when she wanted to could reach a
very high note. Now she let rip with the full power of
her lungs.

For a few seconds the night was torn apart by her
screams, then Luke clapped his hand over her mouth.
'Why, you little . . .' Storm bit his hand and he swore
and hastily took his hand away. But before she had
done more than start to take a breath to scream again
he had put his hand in her hair and jerked her head
back. The next moment his mouth was on hers, his
hands locked on either side of her head as he held her
prisoner.

It didn't start off as a kiss, merely as a means of
shutting her up, Luke's mouth pressed against hers,
effectively silencing her as she struggled to break free.
'You swine,' she muttered against his lips, and tried to
bite him. But Luke wasn't to be caught that way again
and he forced her head back, making her open her
mouth even though she tried desperately to resist
him. He laughed then, in mocking triumph, exploring
the soft warmth of her mouth, taking his time about
it.

At last Luke lifted his head and loosened his hold,
his eyes glittering down at her. Storm took deep
breaths, and as soon as she could speak let fly at him
with all her pent-up rage. 'You worm! You louse! I
could kill you! If you ever dare to touch me again . . .'

'You'll do what?' he asked mockingly.

For answer she let fly at him, hitting out with her
fists. But Luke merely took a step backwards so that

she stumbled and fell against him. He caught her and held her wrists, laughing at the fury and frustration in her face. 'You tigress! Do you want another lesson?'

'You wouldn't dare!' She glared up at him, but her heart began to pound suddenly as she saw a challenging gleam come into his eyes. 'No! I didn't . . .'

But she was saved from any further humiliation as Anne came into the garden and called, 'Storm? Are you there?'

She went to break free of Luke's hold, but he deliberately pulled her to him for a moment and said, in soft menace, 'There'll be another time, lady,' before he let her go.

Turning, she hurried down the path, awkward in her high heels, and ran up to Anne.

'Storm, are you all right?'

'Yes. Yes, I'm OK.' Storm rubbed her wrists and wondered if she looked as if she'd just been kissed against her will. She certainly felt as if it must be glaringly obvious, and she put up a nervous hand to straighten her hair.

'Are you sure? Did Luke find you? I asked him to look for you.'

'Yes, he found me.'

Anne's voice grew a little strained. 'I'm sorry if we upset you by asking you to sing.'

'It's all right.' Storm moved to go back to the bungalow, then hesitated. 'I suppose I should have told you before, but I—I haven't been very well. I've been told not to try to sing for a few weeks.'

'Oh, Storm, I'm so sorry,' Anne said in distress. 'We had no idea. We would have warned them. What is it, a throat infection or something?'

'Oh, no, nothing infectious. It's just strain, that's all.' But she let Anne think that it was her voice that was strained, not her nerves. 'Have they gone?' she asked abruptly.

'Yes, they start work very early in the morning, you see, before it gets too hot.'

Storm sighed as they went into the house. 'You don't have to be tactful, Anne, I know I spoilt your party. I'm sorry. But it was too smoky in there. I just—I just had to get out into the fresh air. I'll help you clear up.'

'Oh no, the houseboy will do it in the morning.' Anne yawned. 'I'm tired.'

'Me too. Goodnight Anne. Say goodnight to Jerry for me.'

Once in the privacy of her own room, Storm's anger returned. How dared that great brute of a man treat her the way he had? A feeling of helpless rage filled her as she thought of all the things she'd like to do to him, and she wished she was a man so that she could hit him and knock him down, then trample on him with her high heels. But the picture this conjured up made her give a high, nervous laugh of tension. Oh, God, this was all she needed, to come to blows with a man who thought it fun to exert his willpower over her. Lying in bed, she wondered if Luke had gone straight to his waiting girlfriend, whether they were even now lying in bed together and he was telling her all about it. Whether they were laughing at her. She gave a small sob of distress and reached out to her bedside cabinet where she had put the bottle of sleeping pills the doctor had given her. But even as she unscrewed the top, Storm's hand hesitated. She had managed without them so far; maybe she could last out one more night. Resolutely she returned them to the drawer and lay back on the pillows, waiting for sleep to come.

It did, eventually, but with it came the nightmare she so dreaded. She was up on stage in a very big concert hall which was packed with fans, the sea of faces beyond the footlights all gazing up at her. The orchestra played the introduction and she opened her mouth to sing, but no sound came out. The orchestra played the introduction again and again, but still she was unable to sing. The audience grew restless, began to shout and boo. Then suddenly their heads came apart from their bodies, became round faces with gaping holes for mouths, mouths that came nearer and nearer, their huge, grinning teeth waiting to tear her to pieces.

Storm woke with a cry of terror, her body wet with sweat, her heart beating painfully. Oh, hell, not again! Knowing that sleep would be impossible for a while, she got up and went to sit in a chair by the window, her feet curled under her. She watched the darkness gradually fade into the golden haze of dawn, the trees and shrubs in the garden brought to glistening life by the sun. At six-thirty she heard quick movements in the house as the boy cleaned up the remains of the party, and at seven she saw Luke come out on to his balcony to eat his breakfast. He was wearing only a pair of shorts, his strong, muscular body tanned and lean, without an ounce of superfluous flesh. There was a mat of dark hairs on his chest, but the rest of him was clean-limbed, contained and powerful. Storm watched him for a few minutes as he stood on his veranda looking out across the hills, but then he turned and sat down as his breakfast was brought to him.

The sight of his strength suddenly made Storm feel weak. She crossed to the bed and stood looking down at the bottle of pills in the drawer of the cabinet, biting her lip, her hands balled into tight fists. Then her hand shot out and she shook out a couple of the pills, swallowing them down before she could change her mind. Quickly she climbed into bed and was soon in the deep, dreamless sleep that only the pills could give.

It was the afternoon before she awoke, but even then she didn't feel refreshed. Her eyelids felt like lead and she kept yawning all the time. For several minutes she just lay there trying to pull herself together, then she dragged herself out of bed to shower and dress, but she could much more willingly have just stayed in bed all day.

Anne was sitting out on the veranda, knitting a minute garment in baby blue.

'Is it going to be a boy, then?' Storm asked as she sat down in a basketwork chair opposite.

'I hope so. I think Jerry would like a boy. Would you like something to eat? I'm afraid you missed lunch and breakfast.'

'No, thanks. Just a drink would be fine. Coffee or fruit juice, please.'

Anne called the boy and then asked Storm what she would like to do that day.

'Nothing really. Please don't feel you have to put yourself out to entertain me, Anne. I'm quite happy to just sit around here.'

'Have you been very ill?' asked Anne. 'The last report

we read about you in the press said that your latest tour was playing to packed audiences and that there was a black market in the tickets.'

Storm·looked at her sister-in-law and gave a rather thin smile. 'Like you, I'm not actually ill, but I don't feel really well.'

Anne looked down at her work, concentrating on an intricate stitch, but her hands became still and when she looked at Storm her eyes were full of tears. 'Oh, Storm, I'm so afraid! I'm sure I'm going to lose the baby.'

Running to her, Storm knelt beside Anne and put her arms round her as she gave a great, convulsive sob and burst into tears. 'I feel so ill! I've been sick every morning for weeks, and the stuff the doctor in Bura gave me hasn't helped, in fact it's made me feel worse. The doctor there isn't any good.'

'Oh, Anne! Oh, my poor darling.' Storm held Anne's head against her shoulder as Anne sobbed heartbreakingly. 'Have you told Jerry?' The other girl shook her head and Storm leant away to look at her. 'But Anne, why ever not?'

'He worries so much. And—and he signed a contract when he took on this job that he'd stay here and see it through to the end. If he doesn't stay he forfeits the bonus Luke has promised him.' Again Anne's body shook with sobs, but she gulped and went on, 'And—and we were relying on that bonus to buy a house and settle down in England. Jerry doesn't want to have to live abroad again now that we're starting a family. If—if I keep the baby.'

'Anne, listen to me.' Storm gently stroked Anne's hair as if she were comforting a child. 'There's really nothing to worry about. You can go back to England right now, if you want to. *I'll* buy you a house. I'd love to do that for you.'

But Anne sat up and shook her head. 'You know Jerry won't accept it. He told me when you offered to buy a house for us before, but he's much too proud to accept.'

'Pig-headed, you mean,' Storm retorted in annoyance. 'But this time I'm not offering the house to him, I'm offering it to you. We won't *ask* him, we'll *tell* him.'

Anne gave a weak smile. 'It's very kind of you, Storm, but it won't be any good. Jerry would hate it, and we'd both be unhappy.'

'Then he's a fool,' Storm said roundly. 'You know I've got more money than I know what to do with. Why shouldn't I spend it on the only family I have left?'

'No, he isn't. He's a man, Storm. He wants to provide for his family himself. It would degrade him to accept such a large sum from you.'

'Even if it means you staying here and perhaps losing the baby?'

'Oh, I don't expect I will,' said Anne, trying to give a cheerful smile. 'I'm just feeling a bit depressed, that's all. You—you won't say anything to Jerry, will you?'

'But Anne, you've *got* to tell him. Surely it isn't fair on Jerry otherwise? I'm sure he'd always put your health first.'

'No.' Anne gave a positive shake of her head. 'I'll be all right, honestly. We've been here this long, it would be stupid not to stay for the last few months. And Jerry has worked so hard, he deserves the bonus Luke has promised him. And then again, I know he'd hate to let Luke down.'

'Oh, Luke,' Storm dismissed him with a gesture.

'What does Luke matter? *You're* the one that we have to take care of.'

'He *does* matter,' Anne insisted. 'If this job is finished on schedule, then Jerry will be able to have more say on the projects he works on, and he'll get a much higher salary. But if he just walks away from the project before it's finished—well, how can Luke be expected to rely on him in the future?'

'But if Jerry explains to Luke, tells him how ill you are?'

Anne shrugged impatiently. 'Oh, Storm don't you see? Luke would just tell Jerry to send me home to England so that my parents can look after me. But Jerry wouldn't leave me. He'd want to be with me.'

'Well, good for him,' Storm said warmly.

'Yes, but not good for his job. Jerry loves this kind of work, Storm, and if he lost this job, or—or gave it up, he'd have a terribly difficult time trying to get another one on the same level. Leaving here and taking me back to England could put his career back at least five years. And all because I'm having bad morning sickness!'

Storm stood up agitatedly, not in the least believing that that was all it was. She didn't know her sister-in-law all that well, but she was sure she wouldn't have cried like that for nothing. 'Is there *nothing* I can do?' she persisted.

Anne smiled and took her hand. 'Just having you here to talk to is enough. But I'm sorry, I've been going on about myself when you're not feeling well yourself.'

'Oh, that's nothing. Nothing,' Storm said dismissively. She held Anne's hand wondering what on earth she could do to help and cursing her brother for being so pig-headed. Couldn't he see that Anne needed to be properly taken care of? But they loved each other so much that they couldn't bear to be parted. She had a sudden inspiration and said, 'Look, Australia isn't that far away and they must have really good nursing homes there. How about if I managed to book you in one for a few weeks so that you could rest and have really good medical attention?' Anne opened her mouth to speak, but Storm held up her hand. 'No, let me finish. I don't know how long it takes to get there, but I'm sure that Jerry could fly over and spend the weekends with you. That way he'd still be able to carry on his job here but see you and make sure that you're all right too. What do you think?' she asked enthusiastically.

Anne hesitated, her face wistful, but then she sighed. 'The dam is behind schedule, Luke would never let Jerry keep having days off to come and visit me.'

'But if he did—would you go?'

Anne nodded. 'Oh *yes*! I so want this baby, Storm. If I lose this one I might never have another.'

'Then we'll have to see what we can do.'

But Anne gripped her hand tightly. 'There's nothing you can do. And remember you promised not to say anything to Jerry.'

Storm hesitated, then said, 'Yes, all right, I won't say anything to him.' She sat back in her chair and after a few moments Anne, satisfied she would keep her word, resumed her knitting. But Storm was far from giving up. She might have promised not to speak to Jerry, but she hadn't promised not to speak to Luke. And she was quite determined to make Luke see just how unfair his working conditions were on her brother and sister-in-law.

As she relaxed in the sun Storm pondered on exactly

what she would say to Luke, but her mind grew tense as she realised that he must already know that Anne was unwell. Jerry himself had told him that Anne was pregnant and Anne had said that Luke kept sending in food parcels for her. To keep Anne happy? Storm wondered. To make Jerry feel even more beholden to him so that he wouldn't leave before the dam was finished? Her face hardened. Of all the underhand tricks! If he was that anxious to have the dam finished on time why couldn't he bring someone else in to take over from Jerry? But after a moment Storm realised that there were lots of arguments against that: Jerry knew all the workers and had welded them into a team, and he got on well with the local people, had even learnt to speak some of their language. As a comparison, Storm could just imagine how it would be if everything had been arranged for her to appear in a one-night show, but then she had backed out so that someone else had to take her place at the last minute. The other person might be a good substitute, but it would hardly be the same. And that applied to Jerry as the Site Director.

So somehow she would have to speak to Luke and get him to agree to let Jerry have several weekends off to visit Anne if she went to Australia. But even if she was successful with Luke, it was going to be far more tricky to get Jerry to agree. Jerry was the kind of person who could only devote his energies to one thing at a time, and that to an almost obsessive degree. He hated having his loyalties divided, which was why he always took Anne with him whenever he went abroad. But Storm was confident that if she emphasised the danger to the baby he would let Anne go. And there was always the chance that if Anne recovered sufficiently she could come back to Taruna to join him.

But first she had to talk to Luke. Anne went inside after an hour or so, but Storm stayed out on the veranda and eventually saw Luke come striding up the path to his bungalow, dressed in a dusty, sweat-stained shirt, jeans and boots, looking exactly like one of the site workers except for the confident way he walked and the arrogant set of his shoulders. As she watched him, Storm vividly recalled the way he had kissed her last night. Having to seek him out and ask him a favour was the last thing she wanted, but the favour wasn't for herself, it was for Anne, and it had to be done.

Storm gave him twenty minutes and then got up and walked across to his house, going round to the front, where she squared her shoulders and determinedly lifted her hand to rap on the door.

CHAPTER THREE

STORM had forgotten about the girl. She had expected Luke to answer the door himself and knew exactly what she was going to say, but when the girl opened it, it threw her completely.

'Er—I'd like to speak to Mr Ballinger, please.'

The girl was beautiful. She looked up at Storm out of large, liquid dark eyes set in a round, dusky-skinned face. She was short and had a curvy kind of figure that looked wonderful on the young but would spread to plumpness before she was thirty. For a few moments the girl just looked at her expressionlessly, then she stepped back and motioned Storm to come inside.

The bungalow was very plainly furnished, with none of the feminine touches that had turned Anne's house into a home. Storm was left standing in the sitting-room for several minutes until Luke came in, his hair still damp from the shower. He had put on clean jeans and a pale blue shirt that was open to the waist. Storm turned to greet him and was immediately aware of his disturbing masculinity, her voice drying in her throat so that she had to clear it before she could speak. And Luke knew it, too, darn him! His mouth curled into a sardonic grin as he said, 'This is an unexpected surprise. Hello, Storm.'

'G-good evening.'

The native girl came in carrying a tray of drinks and

little dishes of nuts.

'Would you like a drink?' asked Luke.

'Please. Gin and tonic, if you have it.'

Luke spoke to the girl in a sing-song kind of language that Storm didn't understand and the girl poured two drinks, added ice, and handed one to Storm with a graceful kind of bow. Storm watched as the girl went on to give Luke his drink, then offered them nuts from the dishes. Storm shook her head, feeling tall and gawky in comparison.

'How nice of you to come and call,' Luke commented with mockery in his voice. 'Won't you sit down?'

'This isn't a social visit,' Storm answered more snappishly than she'd intended. Moderating her tone, she said, 'I'd like to speak to you.'

Luke sat down in an armchair, his long legs stretched out in front of him as he looked lazily up at her where she still stood in the centre of the room. 'Fire away.'

'Alone.' Storm glanced at the native girl, who was hovering by the tray.

'You don't have to worry, Melua doesn't speak English.' Storm just looked at him, and he grinned and sent the girl away. 'All right, so now we're alone,' he said suggestively.

'I want to talk to you about Anne. She tells me that you know she's pregnant.'

A slight frown came into Luke's eyes. 'Yes, I know—Jerry told me.'

'But I don't expect you know how ill it's made her.'

'Ill?' Luke's eyebrows rose. 'No, I didn't. Perhaps you'd better tell me.'

'She's suffering from morning sickness.'

'Don't all pregnant women suffer from that?'

'Possibly, I don't really know. But Anne has it very badly. It's pulled her right down so that now she's depressed and is afraid she's going to lose the baby.'

'Surely there are drugs you can take to stop that kind of thing? I thought Jerry had been taking Anne to see the doctor in Bura?'

'He has, but the stuff the doctor gave Anne didn't help, and now she has no confidence in him. And anyway, it isn't good for a pregnant woman to take too many drugs.'

'So what does Anne want—to go back to England?'

'No. This is Anne and Jerry's first baby. They want to share the experience and be together as much as then can,' Storm explained.

'I see.' Luke sat forward, his glass between his hands. 'So we have a problem.'

'Yes,' Storm agreed, realising that there was no need to go into details; Luke had already seen all the complications Anne's illness implied.

He looked at her, his grey eyes hooded. 'But presumably you've worked something out, or you wouldn't be here,' he remarked drily.

'Can you fly to Australia from here?' asked Storm.

'Not directly, but you can fly to one of the larger islands and get a scheduled flight from there.'

'Would it take long?'

He shrugged. 'A few hours.'

'So if Anne were to go to a nursing home in Australia for a few weeks, Jerry would be able to fly out to see her quite easily—and quite frequently,' she added deliberately.

Luke's lips thinned into a slightly crooked smile. 'So that's what you've worked out!'

'Jerry has worked damned hard for you,' Storm said shortly. 'The least you can do is let him have a few weekends off. If Anne gets really ill, then he'll take her back to England and you'll be left without anyone—despite your food parcels and the bonus you're using to bribe him with!'

Luke's face hardened and he stood up. 'Is that what he said to you?'

'No. But it's easy enough to see. And you're not unobservant, Luke; you must have already realised that Anne is lonely and would rather be in England or somewhere where she could be properly looked after while she's pregnant. She's nearly thirty and this is her first baby, so naturally she's worried. But you want to keep Jerry here, to hold him to his contract, so you send them a few luxury foods as palliatives and to make Jerry feel extra guilty if he lets you down.'

His jaw thrusting forward aggressively, Luke answered curtly, 'Jerry knew the conditions for this job when he signed the contract. We don't encourage our workers to bring their families with them to backward places like this, but Jerry insisted on having Anne with him, so we provided a house for them to live in. And has it occurred to you that Jerry has acted irresponsibly in getting Anne pregnant while he's out here? If he'd waited until the dam was finished there wouldn't have been any problem.'

'You can't always time these things,' Storm answered, a slight flush in her cheeks.

Luke gave her a withering look. 'They're not stupid. They could have planned their family.'

While inwardly agreeing with him, Storm said shortly, 'Well, it's happened, irresponsible or not, so the question still remains: are you going to give Jerry the weekends off to go and visit Anne in Australia?'

'I'll discuss that with Jerry.'

'No, that's not good enough. The suggestion for the whole thing—Anne going to a nursing home and Jerry going to visit her—has to come from you.'

'Are you crazy?' 'Why on earth should *I* suggest such a thing to him?'

'Because otherwise Jerry won't take the time off. He'll think that he's indispensable here and that you won't be able to manage without him.'

'What makes you think I can?'

'It would be very poor policy to have a construction site like this dependent on one man. Jerry could have become ill or had an accident or something at any time. He may be the mainstay of the project, but I'm quite sure you have someone you can fall back on, even if only in the short term,' Storm explained.

Luke gave her a dark look but didn't commit himself. 'So you and Anne have worked all this out between you. Why didn't *she* come and ask me?'

Storm shrugged. 'Maybe she's—in awe of you.'

'Awe?' His eyebrows rose.

'OK, so maybe she's a little afraid of you.' Ignoring his surprised look, Storm swept on, 'What does it matter anyway? Surely all that's important is that Anne is taken care of, and as quickly as possible.'

Luke finished his drink and went over to refill it. He glanced at the glass in Storm's hand, but it was still almost full.

'Are you going to go to Australia with Anne?' he

asked.

'She doesn't want me, she wants her husband.'

'But would you be willing to go with her?' Luke asked, his eyes fixed on her face.

'I've already offered to go back to England with her and put her in her parents' care, but she refused to go so far away from Jerry.'

Luke suddenly put his glass down with an irritable snap. 'Why don't you give a straight answer? I'm not asking if you'll escort her to England, I want to know if you'll stay in Australia with her. Or is your career more important than your sister-in-law's health?' he added sneeringly.

Storm glared at him angrily. 'If she wanted me then of course I'd stay with her, but . . .'

'Good. That's all I wanted to know,' Luke broke in before she could finish. 'All right, I'll talk to Jerry.'

'Now just you wait a minute!' she said angrily. 'You've got to promise not to use my willingness to stay with Anne to persuade Jerry to stay here and not visit her. That isn't what we want at all.' She took a step towards him, her anger rising. 'To do such a thing would be mean and underhand. Not that I'd put it past you to try,' she added scornfully.

Putting his hands on his hips, Luke glared down at her. 'I'm getting more than a little tired of your accusations, lady.'

'I couldn't care less. All I want from you is a promise that you'll let Jerry go and visit Anne as often as he wants.'

'Oh, I promise to speak to Jerry, but what passes between us is nothing to do with you.' Putting out a hand, he took hold of her by the shoulder, holding her at arm's length as she went to step closer and argue with him. 'But there's one other thing I'm going to promise you—and myself. And that's if Anne goes, you go too. I've had enough of you in the last few days to last me a lifetime!'

Storm raised her chin, glaring at him defiantly. 'Well, at least *I'm* not afraid of you!'

He gave a sudden harsh laugh. 'No, there is that. But maybe it would do you good to remember that just because you've made a few records it doesn't give you the right to push people around or try to rule their lives for them.'

'I'm not trying to rule their lives, I'm only trying to help—against ruthless exploiters like you.'

Luke's face hardened in anger and for a moment Storm did feel a frisson of fear that made her spine tingle. His hand tightened threateningly on her shoulder, but he quickly removed it as someone walked past the window and rapped on the door. Turning on his heel, he went to answer it himself, and Storm heard Jerry's voice asking if she was there.

'Yes, she is. Come on in.'

Storm hastily finished her drink and put the glass down as the two men came into the room.

Jerry grinned at her. 'Sorry to interrupt, but we were starting to wonder what had happened to you. Dinner's about ready.'

Glancing at the gold, diamond-framed watch on her wrist, Storm said in a deliberately surprised tone, 'Good heavens, I hadn't noticed the time!' She started for the door, saying casually to Luke as she passed him, 'Thanks for the drink.'

'My pleasure,' he answered, his eyes openly

mocking. 'Maybe we can do it again some time.'

She gave him a brilliant smile, but the look in her eyes ought to have pulverised him into dust. And to add to her annoyance, when they got outside Jerry gave her a knowing grin and said, 'I see you're hitting it off with Luke.'

'Oh, sure,' she replied through gritted teeth. 'Like a house on fire.'

Anne gave her a searching look as soon as they entered the other bungalow, but Storm could only give her a non-committal glance in return. They weren't able to talk until Jerry went out later that evening for his usual last look round the site before turning in.

'You went over to ask Luke to give Jerry time off, didn't you?' Anne demanded as soon as Jerry had gone out of the door.

'Yes, but . . .'

'What did he say, will he let him?'

'I think so, but I'm not entirely sure. God, Anne, trying to get a promise out of Luke is almost impossible! He's as stubborn as a dozen mules and he just wouldn't commit himself. As least he said he'd speak to Jerry, but what the outcome will be I just don't know.'

They had to leave it at that, but the next morning only Jerry was up for breakfast. 'Anne had a bad night,' he explained. 'She's been sick again this morning too. Lord, I hope she's going to be all right. You'll keep an eye on her for me, won't you, Storm?' He stood up ready to go to work. 'Don't hesitate to send for me if you need me. The houseboy will know where to find me.'

'Perhaps the climate and the food here don't agree with her,' Storm suggested.

'It could be. I'll have to take her to Bura to see the doctor again as soon as the plane's available. I'll settle that this morning.'

'Is there only one plane?' she asked.

'No, there's usually two, but one is over in Bura being repaired at the moment. I wonder if Luke wants the plane tomorrow,' Jerry muttered to himself as he left.

Which looked promising, Storm thought. If Jerry asked Luke for the use of the plane and told him why, then Luke would really have no choice but to make the suggestion about Australia. Storm reported this to Anne and the two waited with some impatience until Jerry came home for lunch. He walked into the bungalow with a preoccupied air and at first didn't say anything. For a few furious moments Storm thought that Luke hadn't kept his promise and hadn't spoken to him, but then she noticed that Jerry kept giving Anne rather hesitant glances and thought maybe they would get on better without her there, so she made an excuse to leave them alone together as soon as the meal was finished.

It was quite some time before she heard Jerry leaving to go back to work, then she rushed back into the sitting-room. 'Well?' she demanded. 'What did Jerry say?'

'It worked!' answered Anne, her eyes glowing. 'When Jerry told Luke why he wanted the plane, Luke suggested I might be better off in Australia. Oh, Storm, I can't thank you enough. I'm to go as soon as Luke can fix me up in a nursing home in Darwin. And

Jerry is to take me and he can visit me as often as he wants.'

'Luke's going to choose the nursing home?' Storm asked with some qualms.

'Yes. He has business connections in Australia and spends quite a lot of time there, so it will be easier for him. He's promised to start making enquiries today. Isn't it wonderful? I feel so much happier already.'

Storm had to agree with her, of course, but she didn't trust Luke not to make excuses, to say that he couldn't find a suitable nursing home, just to keep Jerry at the site as long as possible. But she carefully hid this fear from Anne, and the two girls talked over the possibilities for some time until Anne went to her room for a rest. Storm sunbathed for a while, but grew thirsty and went into the house to look for the boy to make her a drink. He didn't seem to be around, so she went into the kitchen, and was surprised to find the dirty dishes from lunch still piled by the sink. Storm hesitated, wondering if it was the boy's day off, but then she took a drink from the fridge and washed the dishes herself, clearing up neatly afterwards.

It came to her as she worked that it was rather quiet. She could hear the birds singing in the garden quite clearly, whereas usually there was the constant background noise of the huge cement-making machines that they used to build the dam.

Feeling restless, Storm decided to take a walk down to the site. Slipping a sundress over her bikini and perching a straw hat on her head, she began to stroll down towards the dam, the dust from the road soon coating her feet and expensive leather sandals with a layer of white powder. She glanced down at her feet distastefully, then stopped and lifted her head as she heard someone shouting. All work on the dam seemed to have stopped, and now that she was nearer she saw that all the men seemed to be gathered in a great crowd near the building where most of the workers were housed. One man was standing on a box or something, and was waving his arms in excited gesticulation as he shouted at the men in a vehement harangue.

Having been brought up in a land dominated by unions, Storm guessed immediately that Luke and Jerry had some sort of industrial dispute on their hands. Curiously she moved nearer, but the man, whom she supposed to be Indonesian, was speaking in a language she didn't understand. Whatever he was saying didn't seem to go down very well with some of the men; they shouted and waved their clenched fists at him, but others took the opposite view and clapped and cheered. Then suddenly it turned nasty as one man pushed at another and they began to fight, their friends rushing to help them.

Storm gasped, foreseeing a riot breaking out, but the next moment Luke stepped forward, lifted the speaker bodily off his box and took his place, giving a great shout that caught everyone's attention.

'Now you listen to me,' he began, and beckoned one of the workers over to translate for him.

After a few moments Storm no longer tried to listen to what he was saying, but became instead absorbed by the way he said it. From the first moment he completely dominated that crowd of men, even though what he had to say had to be translated for him. His strength and toughness came across in the aggressive thrust of his shoulders, in the determined squareness of his jaw. She could see now how he had built himself up to be the head of such a big construction company, it showed in his no-nonsense attitude and the way he had just stepped forward and taken over. It came to her that Luke could probably be very ruthless, especially if he was thwarted in any way.

The men began to talk and mutter among themselves at some suggestion he had put to them, then Luke called for a vote, there was a slow show of hands, and the men turned round and went back to work. It was as simple as that. What looked as if it was going to become a very nasty incident had evaporated beneath the sheer force of Luke's willpower and personality. As the men went back to work in groups, still talking and arguing among themselves, Storm carried on walking towards the site. The Europeans and the foremen were still standing together in a group, obviously discussing what had happened, but as she came nearer, Luke lifted his head and saw her. Quickly he reached out to touch Jerry on the arm and said something to him, so that Jerry detached himself from the group and hurried over to her.

'Is something the matter with Anne?' he asked anxiously.

'No, she's resting. I just thought I'd take a walk down here, that's all. What's going on?'

'Just some internal trouble within the workers' groups: it's happened several times before and it's all over now. They'll be happy for a couple of weeks until they find something else to argue about, I expect.' He began to walk back with her towards the bungalow, saying, 'Perhaps it would be better if you didn't go out walking alone, especially down here. You're probably quite safe, of course, but it might be advisable to wait until I can go with you.' He grinned. 'Or Luke, of course.'

Ignoring that remark, Storm said, 'And does that apply to Anne too?'

'She seldom comes down here, but if she does it's always with me or the houseboy.'

'Is it his day off today?'

Jerry shook his head. 'Wasn't he up at the bungalow? I expect he came down to the dam to find out what was happening. It's amazing how news seems to spread like wildfire around here.'

'Why is there so much trouble?' she queried.

Her brother shrugged. 'Different tribes, different languages, different religions; there are bound to be clashes from time to time. You try to reconcile the basic differences and give them something they all want and it usually sorts itself out. Although this was a pretty sticky problem.'

'Is that how Luke solved it—by giving them something?'

'That's right. He promised them a bonus for every day they finished ahead of schedule, and a big carnival on the day the dam actually opened.'

'He bribed them, then,' Storm commented drily.

Jerry laughed. 'That isn't bribery, that's paying by results. But he threatened them a bit too.' He glanced at her. 'I expect Anne's told you about the nursing home?'

'Yes, I think it's a splendid idea. Just what she needs. She's looking far from well.'

'Yes. She cheered up as soon as I suggested it. The

idiot had been keeping back from me just how bad she was feeling because she was afraid I'd insist on taking her back to England and lose my job.'

'She loves you,' Storm pointed out. 'And she knows this job means a lot to you.'

Jerry nodded. 'And we're at a sticky stage too; so near completion but with all this labour trouble. That's why it's so good of Luke to suggest taking Anne to Darwin. It was Luke's idea, you know. Did Anne tell you that? And Luke's promised that I can go and visit her every other weekend.'

'Big of him,' Storm agreed sardonically.

'Yes, isn't it?' Her sarcasm was lost on Jerry. 'And he's even offered to meet all the nursing home costs.'

Storm's eyebrows rose. 'He has?'

'Yes, but of course I said I couldn't accept it. Anne is my responsibility.'

'Jerry!' She looked at him indignantly. 'If the company offers to pay, then surely . . .'

He laughed at her, his eyes crinkling in his suntanned face. 'It's all right; Luke insisted. He said he didn't want me worrying about Anne instead of concentrating on the job.'

'Now that I believe,' she remarked, cynicism replacing her first surprise. 'But you must keep Luke to his promise, Jerry. The sooner Anne is properly looked after the better.'

'Of course. But Luke never breaks his promises,' he told her in a positive tone. They came to the path leading up to the bungalow and he paused. 'But there's one thing I do regret; Anne's leaving is going to ruin your holiday. You can hardly stay here on your own all day.'

'No, I suppose not.' Storm remembered that Luke had said that if Anne went she must go too, and she wondered if he'd made Jerry promise to get rid of her. For a moment she was tempted to say that she would stay on and see what Jerry's reaction would be, but that would hardly be fair on her brother. 'I'll go when Anne leaves,' she assured him, and was a little hurt to see a swiftly hidden look of relief in his eyes.

He left her, and she walked up to the house and into the garden. Actually she wouldn't have minded staying on here with Jerry. He would be working most of the time, admittedly, but at least she would have got the complete rest that she craved. But then Storm remembered Luke's disturbing presence in the house next door and decided firmly against the idea. Not, she thought grimly, that she would have had any option; Luke would make darn sure that she was off Taruna as quickly as possible.

Lying down on the lounger in her bikini again, she wondered why it was that she had felt such immediate antipathy for Luke. Admittedly they had got off to a bad start, but ordinarily this would have been smoothed over and they would have become sociable, even if not particularly friendly. But Luke's brand of arrogant, domineering masculinity wasn't the type that attracted her. She went for the smoother, more self-possessed type of man, someone who knew how to make a girl feel fragile and cherished. Storm couldn't imagine Luke ever bothering to take that much trouble. He was a man, she guessed, to whom his work would always come first, the company of his male friends over a few drinks second, and women a poor third. So it was little wonder that he kept that girl—what was her name? Melua—to cater for his sexual needs. She was just the sort of woman a man like Luke would want: submissive, obedient, and always available when he needed sex.

Storm's lips curled derisively, and she wondered whether Luke took Melua to all the construction sites or whether he found a new girl for every new project.

'You look as if you're thinking of something nasty.'

Storm opened her eyes to see Luke standing over her. She smiled gleefully. 'Oh, I *was*. I was thinking about *you*.'

'Still your usual charming self, I see,' he returned disparagingly. His eyes went over her in the briefly cut bikini and Storm realised that he wasn't entirely immune to her. 'Well, are you satisfied?'

'Satisfied?' She deliberately raised one knee and let her hand slide gently from it to her thigh, her mouth pouting just a fraction.

Luke's eyes narrowed. 'Now that you and Anne have got what you want.'

She raised her hand to the back of her neck and lifted her thick fall of hair, letting it slowly drift through her fingers. She gave a slight shrug. 'It was Anne who wanted it, not me.' Her pout deepened. 'I don't particularly want to leave.'

She was flirting and she knew it, although she didn't know why. Perhaps it was because Luke was so keen to get rid of her and she wanted to teach him a lesson. Perhaps it was just caprice. But there was no way now that she could stop.

'No? Then what do you want?'

Luke's voice was quite level, and she could read nothing from his features, even his eyes now were completely expressionless. But he couldn't dispel the slight tension in the air that told her that he was fully aware of her. 'I came here for a holiday. You can hardly call the few days I've been here much of a break.'

'So you want to stay on after Anne leaves?'

'It might be an idea,' Storm agreed, looking at him under her lashes.

'When Jerry takes Anne to Darwin he intends to stay there for two or three days to see her settled in.' Luke paused, then squatted down beside her, the material of his jeans stretched tight over his hips. 'You'd be alone here—except for me,' he added deliberately.

'Yes, I suppose I would.' She waited for him to go on, but he just looked at her enigmatically and she realised that he was going to force her to make all the moves. 'But you'd look after me, wouldn't you—if I needed anything?'

He gave a slow smile. 'That might depend on what you needed.'

'Well, if I—got lonely or anything.' Storm's heart had begun to beat rather fast and she knew that this could be dangerous, that she was playing with fire, but something in Luke's eyes held her, challenged her, and she just couldn't stop.

Lifting his hand, Luke deliberately put it on her bare stomach and began to caress her. The skin of his hand was a little rough, it was a hand used to work—and used to handling women too. 'And do you think you might get lonely?' he asked, his voice insinuating.

'I might. Here in a strange country, alone in the

house.'

He leaned forward, his face close to hers, his fingers finding the edge of her bikini. 'In that case I think you really ought to have someone to keep you company.'

'You do? Who would you suggest?' she asked rather unsteadily.

Luke smiled knowingly into her eyes and his hand tightened on her waist. 'How about . . .' He paused and Storm waited for him to commit himself, waited to tell him just what she thought of him and his proposition.

'Yes?' she urged expectantly.

'How about—a nice, fat native woman who'll sit on you every time you make a move towards the door?'

'Why, you——!' Storm sat up and flung his hand away as he began to roar with laughter. He straightened up and Storm too got to her feet. 'If you think I was serious, you're crazy! I was just about to tell you to go to hell.'

Luke's face hardened. 'Do you think I don't know? You're as easy to read as a book—and it's a book I've read more than once before.'

'And just what's that supposed to mean?' Storm demanded, trying to salvage a little of her dignity.

He looked at her scornfully, his eyes again going over her scantily-clad body, but this time there was no appreciation there, only disdain. 'The way you dress and use make-up, the way you do your hair; every bit of it's a come-on. You like to be the centre of attention, to have men look at you and admire you. You like to think that they want you and you can have them any time you want them. That's why you flirted with me just now, because I didn't immediately fall under your spell.' And he laughed again derisively.

Storm went to step angrily past him, but he caught her wrist. 'Oh, no, you don't. I haven't finished yet,' he told her forcefully. The laughter dying, he went on sneeringly, 'But to you it's all a game. You make yourself desirable, but you don't give anything back. You come on strong, but you don't come across. It wouldn't surprise me if under all that act you put on you're nothing but a frigid little virgin.'

She glared at him furiously, too full of rage to speak, and raised her hand to strike him, but Luke's eyes narrowed menacingly and he said, 'Just try it—and I'll put you across my knee and give you the hiding you should have had years ago!'

For a long moment they glared into each other's eyes, Storm's full of impotent rage and Luke's daring her to do anything about it. But then she slowly lowered her hand, admitting defeat, and he nodded, satisfied. But instead of letting her go he said curtly, 'I don't want you coming down to the site again, not alone or with anyone else. It's no place for you. Do you understand?'

Storm nodded, and this time he stepped out of her way so that she could run blindly into the house.

The next morning Luke took off for Bura where there was a radio station, and when he returned the following day he came round to tell Anne and Jerry that he had fixed up a nursing home and that Anne could go as soon as she was ready. Luckily Storm saw him walking up to the bungalow, so she was able to stay in her room until he'd gone; if she never saw Luke again it would be too soon, and now she couldn't wait to leave Taruna to go to Australia with

Anne. But her hopes were doomed to disappointment.
They fixed a day for the three of them to leave, but
when it arrived the other company plane in Bura still
hadn't been repaired, which left only the small one
that Luke had used to bring Storm to Taruna. There
wasn't enough room for Storm to go along with them,
so she had no choice but to stay behind.

'Can't you send a plane to pick me up?' she asked
Jerry as he prepared to leave. 'It doesn't matter how
much it costs, I'm quite willing to pay.'

'I'll try.' Jerry promised rather harassedly. 'Are you
sure you've got everything you want, Anne?'

'Yes, quite sure. Goodbye, Storm. Are you sure
you'll be all right?'

'Yes, of course. Don't worry about me.' But as soon
as Anne's back was turned, she hissed at Jerry, 'Don't
forget—send a plane for me. I don't want to stay here
alone.'

'You won't be alone. Luke's here.'

Storm glared at him. 'Just do as I ask!'

She waited until the plane had circled the site and
watched until it disappeared over the hills, then went
disconsolately back to the bungalow. No plane arrived
to collect her, and at last she gave up watching for
one. She had her time alone here after all, but now
even the idea of being here with only Luke around
was entirely repugnant to her. Not that she had seen
much of him; she had taken care to keep well out of
his way and she did the same now, but he seemed to
spend nearly the whole of his time down at the site.
Apart from helping Anne to pack, Storm had just
lazed around the house and garden, eating and
sleeping a lot, so that the sheen of health was

gradually returning to her skin, the tired, dead look leaving her eyes. At first she had been too dog-tired to be bored, but now that she felt better and Anne and Jerry were gone, the hours started to drag, but she got out her guitar and began to work on the tunes that were drifting into her head. The first day passed and the second; now she could begin to look forward to Jerry's return so that she could leave Taruna, although she still hadn't decided where to go.

On the third day the plant was quiet again as it had been once before. Storm didn't go down this time to find out what was happening, but again there was a lot of shouting and this time the cement-maker didn't start up again. The houseboy hadn't appeared all day so she had to make her own meals. She had her radio on, tuned to Radio Australia, but suddenly the programme of music was replaced by a loud noise of interference. Storm tried to tune it in again, but the noise was blotting out every station and she turned the radio off in disgust. As she did so there was a rap on the front door and she ran to open it. Outside stood one of the half Dutch, half Malay women who lived on the site with their husbands.

'Hello. I come—along you,' the woman said, obviously finding it difficult to speak English.

'Why? What's happening?' Storm let her in and they went into the sitting-room.

'Is—is bad thing. Ballinger—he say me along you.'

Storm tried to find out more, but the woman couldn't tell her anything, could only gesture and then give an expressive shrug of defeat when Storm shook her head helplessly. But the woman kept going anxiously to the window to look out and seemed very worried.

They stayed together for several hours until nightfall,

the woman's anxiety increasing all the time, then there
came a noise like fireworks going off and the woman
jumped up in alarm. 'My—my man. I go.'

'Wait! Where are you going?'

Storm tried to stop her, but the distressed woman ran
out of the house and started down the road towards the
site, her figure soon lost in the darkness. Standing there
rather helplessly looking after her, Storm started to get
angry. How dared Luke send someone who couldn't
speak English? That was just typical of the man. And
why the hell hadn't he come or sent someone to tell her
what was going on? Running back to the bungalow to
fetch Jerry's powerful torch, Storm began to walk down
to the site to find out for herself, indignation overcoming
any uneasiness. Not that she felt particularly afraid; after
all, the other woman had gone down the road only two
minutes earlier, and if she could go, so could Storm.

It was a very dark night, the moon obscured by
clouds, but the road was clearly marked and anyway
there were lots of lights on in the buildings round the
dam site to guide her. The gravel on the road crunched a
little under her sandalled feet, but otherwise it was very
quiet. Even the night creatures seemed to be silent, but
perhaps it was too early for them.

The road had been going downhill and running
parallel with the site, but now it went round a sharp
bend, so that it headed directly towards the dam. Here
some of the native workers had built a small Hindu
shrine on which they had tied scraps of material as
reminders of their prayers. Storm paused in its deeper
shadow to look at the site. She heard several more sticks
of firecrackers going off and wondered if the workers
were celebrating some kind of religious festival, but was

surprised by the absence of any music. She had little knowledge of Eastern culture but she had the definite idea that all festivals were accompanied by lots of music and singing. But it all seemed so quiet except for the firecrackers.

She stood there for a couple of minutes, feeling uneasy and wondering whether to go back, but there was no telephone at the bungalow, no way of finding out what was going on. Slowly now, Storm went on, not yet afraid, but beginning to feel a little apprehensive, the anger that had brought her this far dying. Her eyes tried to probe ahead, but there was no sign of her recent companion, and she could see no one around the buildings at the site. Suddenly all the lights went out together, every one of them, the constant throb of the generator that powered them stilled. She hesitated, wondering what to do, but she was nearer to the first of the buildings than the bungalow now so decided to carry on. Her torch lighting the way, Storm rounded the corner of the first building, the one that contained the explosives and had big red DANGER signs painted on it, then she heard a faint noise behind her. She swung round, the light piercing the darkness, but there was no one there. Then there was a sudden rush of feet from her left and before she could do anything someone grabbed hold of her. The torch was knocked from her hand and she was thrown roughly to the ground.

CHAPTER FOUR

HER ASSAILANT came down on top of her and for a few moments they rolled together in the dirt of the road as Storm tried desperately to get free. But her attacker was a man, big and heavy, and she was no match for his strength even though she struggled wildly. She got one hand free and tore at his face with her nails. He gave a grunt and his hold eased a little. Storm opened her mouth to yell for help, but a hand came over it.

'Don't scream!' the man said urgently in her ear, and Storm's mouth relaxed in astonishment as she recognised Luke's voice. 'Do you understand?'

She nodded and he took his hand away. 'What the hell's going on?' she demanded. 'And why did you knock me down?'

'I didn't know it was you—I thought it was someone after the explosives. And just what are you doing here anyway?' Luke demanded in terse anger. 'I told you to stay in the house with Mrs Sanuri.'

Storm pushed him off her and sat up. 'And just what right do you think you have to tell me what to do? Why couldn't you have sent someone who spoke English? I've been shut up in that house all day, wondering what on earth was happening. You could at least have . . .'

Luke put a hand on her throat. 'For God's sake shut

up!' He stood up and pulled her roughly to her feet. 'Don't you realise we've got a minor revolution on our hands?'

'A revo . . .? Of course I didn't know,' she told him furiously. 'How am I supposed to know anything if you don't tell me?'

'All right, I'm telling you now. Keep your voice down.' Taking hold of her arm he gave her a slight shake. 'Most of the local workers have gone back to their villages, but there are quite a few of the rebels about the site, so we're evacuating the dam until things have quietened down.'

'You mean we're leaving?'

'Yes. I've already sent most of the European workers off to Bura by truck.' Luke had lowered his voice and pulled her farther into the deep darkness of the side of the explosives store. 'They should be safe there and they're armed, they should get through OK.'

'Armed? Is—is it that bad?'

'I told you, it's a revolution,' Luke said roughly. 'Didn't you hear the firing earlier?'

So it hadn't been firecrackers at all. Feeling a fool, Storm could only nod dumbly, but Luke said harshly, 'In that case you were a damned idiot for having come out here. Where's your torch?'

'You knocked it out of my hands,' she reminded him, adding nastily, 'When you did your big he-man act. It must be broken.'

'Well, you'll just have to manage without it. Now listen, you're to go back to the house and pack a few things to take with you to Bura and put them in Jerry's jeep at the side of the bungalow. And you'd better put in some food and drink, just in case we have to hide up somewhere till morning. When you're ready flash the lights of the jeep just once. I'll see them and come up and fetch you. And be as quick as you can, there's a good girl.'

'But I can't see; it's dark. Why can't you come with me now?'

'Because I want to give anyone who's on the lookout for us something else to think about while we get clear of here. Now go on, get going.'

He gave her a little push, but she turned on him fiercely. 'Don't push me around! I don't see why I should go with you, I'm not in any danger, and Jerry will be home tomorrow. So . . .'

'For God's sake, woman!' Luke snapped exasperatedly. 'If you want to stay here and get raped, fine, but just go and get the jeep ready for me first.'

Storm stared at him, suddenly really afraid. She turned to go, but stopped and said, 'Luke, have you got a gun?'

'Of course,' he agreed impatiently. 'Why?'

'I want one too.'

He looked at her, their eyes accustomed to the dark now, and she saw him grin. 'Sorry, no. I'd probably be the first person you'd kill with it. Don't worry, you'll be all right. Now go.'

She ran as fast as she could in the darkness, the sound of her footsteps on the gravel guiding her way, the softness of the grass telling her when she'd gone wrong. It only took her a few minutes to reach the bungalow, and she knew where Anne kept the emergency candles and quickly lit several. Luckily most of her things were still packed, and it didn't take long to shove the others anyhow into the cases and carry them out to the jeep with her guitar. Remembering Luke's instructions about food and drink, she put half a dozen cans of beer and some fruit in the little space left in the back. Satisfied that she'd got everything, Storm had a couple of bad moments when she realised that she needed the keys to turn on the ignition, but luckily she remembered that there was a row of hooks with keys on them by the front door, and there were the keys for the jeep, clearly labelled.

Putting on her jacket, she blew out the candles, closed the door of the bungalow and locked it, a silly thing to do in the circumstances, but it was still Anne and Jerry's home. Turning on the ignition, she switched on the lights and counted to ten, hoping that was long enough and Luke had seen them. She waited expectantly, but he didn't appear, and she began to be afraid that he hadn't seen the signal—or that something had happened to him. Fear began to feed her imagination, and the cry she gave when Luke suddenly loomed out of the darkness beside her was one of both relief and fright.

'Quiet!' he ordered in an angry whisper. 'Do you have to scream all the time?'

'You frightened the life out of me! Where have you been?'

'Getting a few things from my place. Are you all set?' He went to put a hold-all into the back and found that there wasn't any room. 'What on earth are all those cases?' he demanded.

'My clothes, of course.'

Luke swore infuriatedly. 'I told you to bring a *few* things!' He began to heave her cases out and drop them on the gravel.

'Hey! What do you think you're doing? I'm not leaving those behind,' Storm told him in a furious undertone.

'All right, stay with them, then. That would suit me just fine.'

'You beast! Don't you *dare* throw that guitar on the ground!' Her voice had enough menace to make him stop and he placed it gently on the grass.

'Did you put some food in?' Storm nodded and he said, 'How about some blankets?'

'Why no, I . . .'

'All right, I'll get some.' He went to go in the bungalow, but found it locked and raised his eyes to heaven. 'My God—women!' Turning, he went back to his own house and returned carrying several blankets which he dropped on the back seats. Then he spotted a small case that Storm had put back. 'I told you no excess baggage. I've left you one case,' he said furiously, and went to throw it out again.

Storm grabbed the locked blue leather case and held on to it. 'It's my jewel case. I worked damned hard for these, and if you think I'm going to leave these as well as my clothes behind to be pawed over by a lot of dirty revolutionaries . . .'

Her voice rose hysterically and Luke quickly put his hand on her arm. 'All right, all right. Just get in the jeep.'

Pushing her into the passenger seat, he got in beside her and let off the handbrake so that the vehicle rolled gently and silently forward.

'Aren't you going to put on the lights?' Storm asked nervously, clutching the sides.

'Can't risk it yet. Don't worry, I know the path like the back of my hand.'

They glided down, the little stones that came up and hit the underside of the jeep sounding like pistol shots in the echoing darkness, so that Storm grabbed Luke's arm and almost made him swerve off the road. 'What's that?'

'Let go!' Dragging his arm free, Luke managed to straighten up the jeep and swore again. 'Of all the bird-brained females!' They came to the little shrine and he pulled up and jumped out.

'Where are you going?' Storm demanded in a fright, preparing to follow him.

'It's all right, I left some extra petrol here.' He loaded it in the back and got in again. 'Right, now keep down and for God's sake keep quiet. The next bit might be tricky.'

Storm glared at him but got down on the floor. 'Do you realise this thing is lethal?' she hissed at him. 'If a bullet hits that petrol we'll go up like a bomb!'

'Shut up!' he hissed back, the jeep going more slowly on the less steep gravel.

Peering over the bottom of the windscreen, Storm saw the dark bulk of the explosives store drift past. The jeep went on for another hundred yards and then Luke steered it on to the grass and stopped. 'What are you going to do?' she asked.

Luke grinned at her. 'Create a diversion so that we can get away. Cover your ears.'

Going over to a nearby tree, he moved away some branches of scrub and leaned forward. Suddenly there was an almighty explosion behind them, and Storm cried out in terror as the explosives store blew up. At

the same time another building went up in a great
burst of flame, lighting up the whole of the site, and
burning so fiercely that she guessed it must be the fuel
store. Running to the jeep, Luke jumped in and
started the engine.

'What have you done?' she shouted at him.

'Stopped them from blowing up my dam!' Gunning
the accelerator, he drove furiously down the road that
went through the site.

There was a shout, then more, and Storm glimpsed
some men running towards them, their figures
macabre in the light of the flames that lit high into the
sky. 'Look out, you'll hit them!' she yelled in alarm.

But Luke put a hand on her head and pushed her
down, at the same time pressing the accelerator to the
floor. There was the sound of firing again, only much
nearer, and Luke swore, the jeep swerving a little as
bullets rang against its thick steel bodywork. Storm
didn't dare look up, could only crouch on the hard
bucketing floor that bruised her hips, and cling on as
they raced out of the light of the burning building and
into blessed darkness again.

Luke switched on the headlights and kept going for
a good ten minutes before he slowed and pulled up in
the shelter of some trees. 'Hell and damnation!' he
exclaimed.

Pulling herself swiftly up into the seat, Storm glared
at him. 'Don't you ever stop swearing?'

'Sorry, lady, but this is no Sunday School outing,'
he told her with sarcastic scorn. He got out and
started searching in the back. 'Where's the first aid
box?'

'What first aid box?'

'Oh, great!' He straightened up. 'I suppose you're trying to tell me you didn't put it in.'

'Why should I? You didn't tell me to.'

'Damn typical female!' He yanked out his holdall and began to unzip it.

'Look, I'm just about fed up with you always going off at me! If you don't . . .' Her voice broke off as she stared at his hand. 'Your hand! There's—there's blood on it.'

'So why do you think I wanted the first aid box? I'll have to tear up this shirt.'

He began to pull at it, but Storm took the shirt from him. 'I'll do it. Is it bad?'

'I don't think so. It's only my arm.' He undid his shirt and shrugged it off, revealing a deep graze in the upper part of his left arm which was bleeding freely. 'If I wash it and bandage it, it should be all right.' He looked at her. 'You did bring some water, didn't you?' Then he sighed resignedly. 'I thought not.'

'You told me to bring something to drink, so I brought beer. How was I to know you were going to get yourself shot?' Storm demanded, letting anger cover her relief that he wasn't badly hurt.

Reaching into his holdall again, Luke produced a bottle of whisky. 'Here, clean it with that—and don't waste any! But first tear the shirt into strips to make a pad and bandages.'

'I know what to do,' Storm informed him crossly. 'I've seen plenty of Westerns.'

To her surprise he gave a low chuckle which turned to a smothered wince of pain as she applied the whisky and bandaged his arm. When she'd done Luke slowly let out his breath. 'I've an idea you enjoyed that,' he told her through gritted teeth.

'Don't be stupid.' Storm found that her hands were shaking so she picked up the whisky bottle and took a drink. 'Lord, I needed that!'

'Your concern to put your patient's needs before your own is touching,' Luke said sardonically, and took the bottle from her to take a long swallow himself. Putting his shirt back on, he said, 'Right, let's get going. I want to put as much distance as I can between us and the site.'

They drove on, but it became increasingly difficult when Luke turned off the main road into a track that went off to the right, although the so-called main road had been hard enough where it had been churned up by heavy lorries bringing supplies to the dam.

'Why have you turned off?' Storm demanded.

'The main road goes through a village and I'd rather not chance the reception we'd get there.'

'But I don't understand why all this has happened. If there's political unrest on the island why should it affect us? And why on earth should they want to shoot at you when you've brought so much work to the place? Don't they want the dam or to have electricity?'

'They're so backward here a lot of them don't care. And a lot of people will lose their land when the dam's flooded,' Luke told her above the noise of the engine. 'But the main reason is that the rebels are trying to overthrow the local government on the island, and it's the government that allowed us to come in and is largely paying for the dam. They want the benefits to bring them into line with the other islands in Indonesia, but it's a lot for them to pay for, so it's easy for the rebels to move in. And they see me and my men as agents of the government, I suppose.'

He concentrated on the road as they drove on, but it was so bad that several times he lost it entirely and they had to go back. After three hours when they had covered only a few miles, Luke drew up. 'It's no good, we'll have to wait until morning. It ought to be safe enough here, but we'd better keep watch just in case someone has tried to trail us. You'd better try and get some sleep in the back.'

'No.' Storm shook her head firmly. 'You sleep, I'll keep watch.'

'And have you scream every time a cricket chirps! A fat lot of rest I'd get!'

'I won't scream—unless I have to,' Storm said steadily.

Luke looked at her for a moment, then nodded. 'All right.' He took the blankets from the back and gave her one. 'If you feel yourself falling asleep don't try to keep awake, just wake me up and I'll take over.' Wrapping the blanket round himself, he lay down beside the jeep on his right side and was soon asleep.

Storm put the blanket on the grass beneath a tree and leaned against the trunk, her eyes and ears alert, and feeling far more nervous of any creatures that might come near her than the rebels. She wished she had the gun to hold, she would feel more confident if she knew she had something to defend herself with, and she looked across at Luke's sleeping figure, wondering if she could get it out of his belt without waking him. He was sleeping deeply and she guessed worriedly that he must have lost quite a lot of blood. It must have really taken it out of him to drive in the dark over this terrible road for the last few hours.

A sound in the grove of forest behind them made her hair stand on end and she sat tensely, her arm reaching out ready to grab Luke if it came any nearer. But the sound wasn't repeated and she very slowly relaxed. She also thought she heard a sort of dripping sound, but it was so soft and so continuous that it didn't alarm her, although she couldn't think what it was; perhaps sap dripping from a tree on to the grass, she guessed, but she was unfamiliar with the flora on the island and couldn't be sure. Once Luke turned over in his sleep and woke with an indrawn breath of pain as he lay on his bad arm. 'Storm?' he said quickly, softly.

'Yes, I'm here.'

'Everything OK?'

'Yes, fine.'

'Are you tired? Do you want me to take over?'

'No. Go back to sleep.'

He didn't argue, just turned back to his right side and seemed to go instantly asleep. Storm envied him the ability; admittedly she was feeling much better now than she had for ages, and she hadn't had the nightmare for nearly a week, but she didn't think she would be able to sleep in circumstances like these however tired she was.

Morning came at last, and came quickly once the first faint light of dawn broke through the deepness of the night. Storm had often lain awake in the last months, watching the darkness fade, but it had always been in a bedroom somewhere, never out in the open like this. Now she watched the brilliant, breathtaking transformation of night into day, saw with what a dazzling display of colour the *aubade* of dawn blazed across the sky. She watched and marvelled, and felt suddenly humble and privileged to see such beauty and magnificence. She couldn't think why she hadn't sat up to watch the dawn before, and decided that when this was over and she was back in England she would get up very early to watch it as often as she could. But even as Storm made the resolution she knew she wouldn't keep it. Once she started working again there would be so many late shows, so many showbiz parties, so many public appearances, and she would get tired again and forget all about the wonder of the dawn. The only time she would probably see it would be a glimpse from a car window on the way home from a party that had gone on all night, and then she would just be longing to go to bed and close her eyes to the day.

She felt suddenly dispirited, not looking forward to the future at all. But then the blood-red orb of the sun appeared over the horizon, and she knew that no matter what happened she would always have this one perfect dawn to remember.

It was light enough now for her to see her surroundings. Behind them were groves of trees that thickened into forest as the ground rose higher, and in front the road and beyond it a long valley of wet fields, their waters glinting dazzlingly in the morning sunlight. Storm looked carefully, but could see no sign of any houses or people; there weren't even any animals in this remote place.

Luke stirred a little and she turned to look at him, hoping he felt better. His face still looked hard even when he was asleep, his square jaw jutting forward as if he was defying even his dreams. Was there no softness about him? she wondered. Had he so little regard for women that he had never wanted to marry, or have a family? Perhaps this company that he had built up from nothing was all the solace that he needed. It must certainly give him enough excitement and challenge. Last night, when he had blown up the explosives rather than let them be used to destroy the dam, he had called it *his* dam. So it must give him a lot of satisfaction to see it being built, the sort of satisfaction other men would get from building a loving marriage or from raising a child. And for his bodily appetites there would always be girls like Melua.

For the first time Storm wondered what had happened to her. Had Luke sent her back to her family? But surely if she had been known to be his mistress wouldn't that be dangerous for her now? She ought to be here with Luke, escaping with him instead of me, Storm realised uneasily. Did he care so little about the girl that he had just let her get away and hide as best as she could?

The sun touched Luke's face and he yawned and sat up, looked round and met Storm's accusing eyes. 'Hi.'

'You louse!' she said witheringly. 'If you cared enough about the girl to go to bed with her you could at least have brought her with you.'

He blinked and shook his head rather dazedly. 'Did I miss something somewhere?'

'I'm talking about Melua. Why didn't you bring her with you?'

Getting to his feet, Luke started to roll up the blanket. 'Why should I?'

'These rebels—if they want to get back at you, then

they might try to hurt anyone associated with you.'

'Melua's safe enough,' he said shortly, and strode to the jeep to take out a can of beer. 'Where's the food?'

'How do you know she's safe? Did you make sure? Surely you owe her that much at least,' Storm demanded, getting stiffly to her feet.

Picking up a cardboard box, Luke looked into it and said angrily, 'Is this all the food you brought? Two packets of biscuits and some fruit?'

'What did you expect—a Harrod's hamper?' They glared at each other, the jeep between them. 'Well?' Storm persisted. 'Why didn't you bring her with us? She was always on hand when you wanted her, wasn't she? As your mistress she had the right to be taken care of. What did you do—just pay her off and tell her to get lost?'

'I didn't tell her anything,' Luke answered shortly, tearing open the beer can. 'And she isn't my mistress. Who told you she was?'

'But she was living with you,' said Storm, taken aback.

'She was *working* for me. And her brother took her away as soon as the trouble started.' He added sardonically, 'And her brother, in case you didn't know, is Jerry's houseboy.' Storm's mouth formed into an O of surprise. 'Exactly. And if you're thinking that he sold her services to me, then you're wrong about that too.'

She glowered at him, somehow annoyed that he hadn't been proved to be a louse. Rolling up her blanket, she threw it in the back of the jeep. 'I'm going for a walk.'

'Stay within sound of the jeep,' he warned her. 'You

might get lost.'

'I'm not that stupid,' she answered acidly.

'No?' he said derisively. 'And I'm not that lucky.'

She gave him a killing look that only made him laugh and walked through the trees until she came to a little stream that trickled down from the hills. There wasn't much water in it, but enough to wash her face and top half after she'd taken off her shirt. The sun soon dried her and she walked back feeling refreshed and more amiable, even rather pleased now that Melua hadn't been Luke's mistress after all.

He was having a shave with an electric razor connected to the jeep's battery, using the wing mirror to see his reflection. Storm stood for a moment watching him, and into her mind came the memory of the kiss he had given her. He was so much of a man, so big and so broad, so strong and hard. And he was so much more of a man than anyone she'd ever met before. Perhaps because he so enjoyed his masculinity; he liked to use his hands as well as his brain, to be clean but not care if he got dirty, and he had thoroughly enjoyed blowing up half of Taruna and that mad ride through the site with bullets flying at them out of the darkness. And he would know how to make love, Storm was sure of that. He would handle women as easily and as casually as he did everything else. And leave them happy? Perhaps. But he would always leave them. So maybe it was just as well that they wouldn't be alone for very much longer.

Luke finished shaving and turned to look at her quizzically, as if he'd known that she was watching him. 'Do you want any breakfast?' he asked.

'No.' She shook her head and stepped forward.

'How's your arm?'

'Fine. Thanks for keeping watch for so long.'

'That's all right.' She felt suddenly shy. 'Would—would you like me to look at it?'

'No, I think it'll be OK. There's a hospital in Bura, I'll get them to check it there.'

He moved to get in the jeep, but Storm felt that she didn't want to go, not yet. 'Is it likely to be dangerous any more?' she asked.

Luke shrugged. 'It's hard to say. We only had the radio link with Bura and the first thing the rebels did was to smash the transmitter. I don't really know whether the insurgents were among our workers and it started there or whether the whole island is in rebellion. But there's a big fortress in Bura that houses all the administration buildings, and that should be able to hold out for quite a time. Long enough, anyway, for a peace-keeping force to be sent over from Jakarta. But the sooner we get to Bura the better, I think.'

'Yes, of course.' Storm walked to the jeep and put one foot in it, then paused, looking at the view of the hills and sparkling valley. 'It's very beautiful here, isn't it?'

'Most of the world is beautiful. It's only man who ruins it, who desecrates and kills his own environment.'

'Doesn't building dams desecrate the landscape?' Storm asked, but without mockery.

'Yes, it does,' Luke agreed, to her surprise. 'But they also make arid places fertile and bring energy and modern amenities to backward people.'

'So that they can all sit in their huts and watch

television!' and now Storm's voice was derisive.

'That's right. They can all watch you performing in your latest show and listen to your records on their radios,' Luke answered shortly.

She bit her lip and looked away, then said huskily, 'I'm sorry. I suppose everyone has their job to do.'

'*You? Apologise?* I don't believe it.'

Storm turned angrily, ready to snap at him, but saw only laughter in his grey eyes and realised that he was teasing her. She smiled reluctantly, and Luke shook his head. 'Ah, now you shouldn't have done that, you know.'

'Done what?'

'Smiled. Now I shall have to start revising my opinion of you again.'

'Again?'

'Mm. I just get you nicely slotted and you do something that makes me change my mind about you.'

Intriguing. Storm hadn't realised that he thought about her at all. 'And what was your first opinion of me?' she couldn't resist asking.

Luke laughed. 'Now that's a question you would have been much wiser not to ask.'

'Not good, huh?'

'Terrible.' He got in the jeep. 'I'm afraid we have to leave now.'

So he understood. Getting in beside him, Storm said, 'I watched the dawn break. I've never really looked at it before.'

Luke looked round and nodded. 'Yes, this is the perfect place for it. I wish I'd shared it with you,' he said sincerely. But then he started the jeep and they drove on.

The road was very rough, not much more than a track which had been churned up in the rainy season and dried into hard ruts that made their teeth rattle and their bones ache. Luke drove as fast as he could, but Storm noticed that he kept looking in the mirror the whole time to make sure they weren't being followed. He kept looking, too, among the trees at the side of the road, especially when they came very close.

She should have felt nervous, but she didn't, and she ought to have felt tired, but she was fully awake, even enjoying the ride after having spent so much time just lounging around the bungalow. They went down an incline, splashed through a muddy stream at the bottom and started to climb up the other side, when the engine began to cough and splutter and smoke poured from under the bonnet.

'What the . . .' Jamming on the handbrake, Luke jumped out and ran to lift the bonnet. Immediately clouds of steam billowed out and he sprang back. 'The radiator's dry! How the hell did that happen? I checked it before we left and it was . . .' He was squatting down, examining the radiator, and gave an exclamation. 'A bullet-hole! A ricochet from the road, by the look of it.' He stood up, frowning. 'That's strange, it must have been dripping out all night. But surely you would have heard it?'

Storm shook her head. 'No, I didn't hear a . . .' She stopped, remembering what she thought had been sap dripping from a tree. 'Oh.'

Putting his fists on his hips, Luke gave her a scornful look. 'What did you think it was—a solitary drop of rain? If you'd wakened me I would have been able to plug it.'

'Well, can't you plug it now?' Storm demanded, her amiability vanishing.

'Sure, but what would be the point? The engine has probably blown its guts out, and even if it hasn't we don't have any water to put in the radiator—thanks to you.'

Standing up in the jeep, she glared back at him. 'How was I to know you were going to be stupid enough to drive through a hail of bullets? And you're the one who got the jeep ready—*you* should have put in a spare water can.' And she sat down triumphantly, feeling that she'd got the better of that argument.

Coming to the side of the jeep, Luke took out his holdall and the food and drink, which he put inside the bag. 'I don't know what you're sitting there for,' he said nastily, 'because that jeep isn't going any further.'

Storm stared at him. 'What do you mean? Aren't you going to fix it? Surely we can get some water from that stream.'

'I can't work on the engine until it cools down, and right now it's burning hot. And even then I'm not sure that I could fix it for long enough to get us to Bura.'

'Of course you could,' she interrupted. 'You're an engineer, aren't you? You can fix anything.'

He gave a grim smile. 'A civil engineer and a motor mechanic aren't necessarily one and the same. Even if I could repair it, it would take most of the day, and I don't want to hang around here that long.'

'But you can't—can't just abandon it,' she protested in dismay.

'Well, that's what I'm doing. But if you want to phone a garage and wait for them to send out a repair truck to fix it, that's your privilege,' he said sarcastically.

She gave him a fulminating look. 'All right, I get the message. Will we be able to hire a car in the next village?'

Luke raised his eyes to heaven. 'Don't you ever learn? There are no telephones, no garages, no rent-a-car. We're going to have to *walk* the rest of the way.'

'How far is it?' she asked, dreading the answer.

'About fifty miles or so.' He looked at her appalled face and added mendaciously. 'That's as the crow flies, of course. We're not so lucky. We have to go up and down and around the hills.'

'But I can't possibly walk that far!'

'OK, so stay here. I'll send some transport back for you when I get to Bura. And I'll travel much faster on my own.' And Luke picked up his holdall and started up the hill.

'Wait! You can't possibly leave me here alone. You said yourself it might be dangerous. You've got to *do* something!'

He turned back to her. 'What *can* I do? Whistle up a taxi? You either walk with me and keep up with me or you're on your own.'

Storm looked at him furiously but climbed out of what now seemed the haven of the jeep. 'Oh, all right! Let me get my things.' She lugged out her suitcase and her jewel case, then rather defiantly unearthed her guitar from where she'd hidden it under the spare wheel.

Luke gave her a look, but said, 'Let's get moving.'

'All right, if you'll take my case, I'll carry my jewels

and the guitar.'

He gave her a nasty grin that she was beginning to hate. 'You want them, you carry them.'

'You pig! It wouldn't hurt you to help me.' But he just stood there, so Storm bent to open the case and then let out a cry of dismay. 'Oh, no! You fool! You put the wrong case in. This one has only got some of my show dresses in it. Now I haven't even got a toothbrush or any make-up or . . .'

'Good, then you won't mind leaving it behind,' Luke said sourly. 'Will you please hurry up?'

Angrily she relocked the case and put it back in the jeep in the feeble hope that it might still be there when she was able to send someone back for it. She put the guitar across her shoulders and picked up her jewel case. 'Don't forget the blanket,' Luke warned, so she picked that up too, and set out after him as he began to climb the hill.

'Shouldn't we try to move the jeep off the road?' she panted as he strode ahead.

He looked back. 'There isn't anywhere to hide it. And if anyone's following us, they'll know we're on foot soon enough.'

Storm looked at him with troubled eyes. 'Do you really think they will?'

'They might. They know I'm the head of the construction company, and they probably know that you're rich, the way you've been flaunting those jewels around the place. The rebels might think it would be worth their while to hold us hostage—that's a pretty popular pastime around the world nowadays. And I'd just as soon not give them the opportunity. So come on.'

He strode on, and Storm followed as best she could in

her high-heeled sandals, the guitar bumping against her back as she tried to hurry along.

'Luke! Wait!' He stopped and she came panting up, her clothes already clinging to her as she perspired in the heat. 'This is ridiculous. It's going to take ages to get there. Isn't there a better road than this?'

'No, not for a few miles.' He looked disparagingly down at her feet. 'I'm not surprised you can't walk, in those silly shoes. 'Haven't you got any others?'

'You know darn well I haven't!' Storm yelled at him, her temper snapping. 'You put the wrong case in the jeep. If I'd known you were going to make me walk the whole way I'd have worn my hiking boots!' she shouted scornfully.

Luke's face hardened. 'Why don't you be sensible and throw the guitar and the jewels away? They're not going to do you any good, and you'll end up by throwing them anyway.'

'No, I'm taking them with me. And if you were even remotely like a gentleman you'd carry one of them for me,' she told him through gritted teeth.

He gave a harsh laugh. 'Too bad, lady, you picked the wrong man. If they mean so much to you, then you hang on to them—until they get so heavy that you hate the sight of them and throw them away yourself!' And he turned and began to walk on again in his sturdy boots.

'You louse! You rotten swine!' Storm shouted at him. But he just laughed and strode on.

Picking up her things, she struggled after him, cursing the fates that had put her in this rotten situation and cursing them even more for making Luke the man she had to share it with.

CHAPTER FIVE

STORM soon lost all interest in the scenery. All she could see was the track stretching ahead in front of her and Luke's boots taking the ruts in his stride. When he got a few hundred yards ahead, he would stop and wait for her to come up, his eyes amused as he watched her struggling along. And as soon as she reached him he would start off again, so that she had no chance to rest. Storm began to hate the sight of his broad back in the distance. And those boots! God, how she hated him for having those boots.

They had started off very early, but as the sun rose the day grew hotter, making Storm perspire and get hot and thirsty. Pausing to wipe the sweat from her face, she looked longingly at the holdall, carried so easily in Luke's strong hands, but he didn't stop and take out a can of beer until ten o'clock when they had been walking for almost four hours. She collapsed on to the grass, her back against a tree trunk in the blessed shade, almost giddy from exhaustion and panting for breath. Luke handed her a can of beer and she drank greedily.

'Take it slowly,' he warned her. 'Just sip it at first.'

But she took no notice of him and took the warm, fizzy liquid down in great gulps, but gave herself hiccups.

'I told you,' Luke said mildly, sitting down beside her. 'Take deep breaths.'

'Oh, shut up!' Storm retorted angrily, and helped herself to a biscuit and a banana. 'How far have we come?' she asked when she'd finished eating and the hiccups had subsided.

'About five or six miles, I should think.'

'Is that all! At that rate it will take us *days* to get to Bura!' she exclaimed in consternation.

Luke didn't answer, just looked at her expressively, and she turned away. Her shoulder felt raw where the strap of the guitar case had rubbed and her hips and back were bruised where it had bumped against her. She would have to do something, she realised, she couldn't walk fifty miles like this, but that guitar was the first one she had ever owned, the one she had composed her first hit songs on, and it meant a lot to her. She was darned if she was just going to abandon it if she could possibly avoid it. But the guitar was one thing, the case was another. Storm decided she could quite easily abandon the case, and wondered why she hadn't thought of it at the start. But Luke had been in such an all-fired hurry that he hadn't given her time to think.

Taking the guitar from the case, she carefully wrapped it in the blanket, as much to protect her from being knocked as to protect the guitar.

'You're crazy,' Luke told her roundly. 'You can buy yourself another dozen guitars once we get out of this.'

'There aren't any like this one,' she said fiercely. 'This one's special. It took me months to save up for it and take lessons. Having it transformed my whole life.'

She looked up at him and found him watching her with an expression she hadn't noticed in his face before; as if he found her interesting. 'You're full of surprises,' he commented, and made no more objections to her taking the guitar.

From that, Storm turned her attention to the jewel case, realising that if she wore the jewellery, she wouldn't have to carry the case any more. Cases, she was beginning to realise, were encumbrances, it was what was in them that mattered. So she unlocked the case and took out the smaller cases inside, opening them one by one, and putting on the bracelets and necklaces, the rings and a couple of pins. The earrings she put into the pocket of her shirt, together with a couple of rings she had no fingers left for.

Luke watched her in fascination and when she'd finished roared with laughter. 'You look like a walking display stand out of Tiffany's! And I suppose all those pieces are precious to you too, are they?'

'Some of them,' Storm admitted, the diamond pendant at her throat catching the sun and reflecting its rainbow prism on the soft skin of her neck. 'Don't you have anything that's precious to you? That you couldn't bear to lose?'

The corner of Luke's mouth twisted into a wry grin as he shook his head. 'No. Nothing.'

He said it so definitely that she was shaken. 'That isn't much to say for a whole life.'

'I'm not acquisitive,' he answered shortly. 'I like to travel light. I don't see any point in buying things just because everyone else has them.'

'Don't you have a home? A base?'

'I have a service flat near our offices in London, but I don't spend very much time there. I'm usually travelling around making sure that projects are running smoothly, or else chasing up more construction jobs.'

'Don't you have any family?'

Luke shook his head. 'No one close.' He gave her one of his quizzical, slightly derisive looks. 'How about you, where do you live?'

'Basically in London, I suppose, but I have a beach house in California as well.' Not that she saw much of either place, Storm thought dispiritedly, there never seemed to be the time. She always seemed to be catching a plane to jet off to another engagement, to make another recording. This was the first real holiday she'd had in years and she had to land in the middle of an uprising! Taking off her shoes, she rubbed her ankles, which ached from having to walk on such uneven ground. She was lucky that she hadn't already wrenched an ankle or even broken one. 'Do you have a knife?' And when he raised an interrogative eyebrow, 'I want to try and lower the heels on my sandals.'

'Here, I'll do it for you.' Taking a clasp knife from his pocket, Luke opened it and began to work on the wedge-shaped heels of her shoes. 'Do you have anyone other than Jerry?' he asked after a couple of minutes.

Storm thought fleetingly of Wayne and realised how little she missed him now. 'No, not really.'

He gave her a quick glance. 'Your world is so completely different from mine. Do people in show business ever get married nowadays?'

'Only as often as they get divorced,' she answered flippantly. 'And divorce is so messy that it's easier not to marry.'

'So what do *you* do?'

Storm had been watching him working deftly on her shoes, but now she lifted her head to find his eyes on her intently. A wave of physical awareness swept over her, making her acutely conscious of the thin shirt sticking to her breasts, and the fact that she'd pulled her skirt up to her thighs to cool her legs. A fear of her own reaction filled her and she said shortly, 'Me? Oh, I don't do anything. I'm frigid, remember? Have you finished my shoes?'

He tossed them to her but said, 'Frigid—or afraid?'

She gave a short laugh. 'I'm nearly twenty-five years old and I've been in show business for years—can you really imagine that there's anything I *haven't* done?' It wasn't true, but somehow Storm felt goaded into saying it. Because Luke was right, she did feel afraid. Not of him exactly, but of getting involved with him. Feelings she didn't really understand herself.

'I don't believe that,' Luke said flatly.

'Don't you? You should.' She looked away, wondering why she occasionally felt nervous of him. Most of the time she disliked him intensely, especially when he treated her like an idiot, but there were times—like now—when she was so sexually aware of him that she felt vulnerable and afraid. 'Can I borrow your knife?'

He handed it to her, closed again, and laughed when she broke a nail and swore. Storm turned and came up on her knees, the open knife in her hand and real anger in her eyes. 'Don't you *dare* laugh at me!' she snapped furiously.

Luke made one movement, so swift that she could hardly follow it, and caught her wrist, squeezing until she dropped the knife. 'And don't *you* ever dare threaten me again,' he said acidly, his angry eyes burning into hers.

Storm bit her lip and looked away. 'I wasn't . . . I didn't mean to threaten you with it. I just happened to be holding the knife when you made me mad, that's all.'

'What the hell is it with you?' he demanded, in no way mollified and still holding her wrist. 'What were you running away from when you came here?'

'Running?' She gave a puzzled shake of her head. 'What makes you think that? I just needed a rest, that's all.' For a moment blue eyes met grey, but then Storm dropped hers and said, 'Can I have the knife back now?'

'What do you want it for?'

'To cut a strip off my skirt to make a ribbon.' He gave it to her and she cut a couple of inches up the hem of her skirt, then tore it off, using the strip to tie her hair back off her face. Carefully and awkwardly she closed the knife and handed it back to Luke.

'If you'd any sense,' he told her, 'you'd have cut your hair off instead. You'd have felt a whole lot cooler.'

'Why? Don't you like my hair?' she exclaimed, shocked, and hardly able to believe her ears. Men always raved about her hair. Wayne always referred to it as a golden mane whenever he did a press hand-out.

Luke laughed at her consternation and got to his feet. 'You ready to move on?'

She wasn't, but there was no way she was going to plead with him, so she put on her shoes and slung the guitar across her back again. It was much lighter and more comfortable now, and walking was easier too, so that they made better progress. Luke had put his arms through the straps of the holdall and carried it like a backpack, the blanket fastened to it, so that he had his hands free. Storm walked beside him for a mile or so, but then the heat got her again, and she began to feel the lack of any sleep last night. She started to lag behind, but Luke took her hand and helped her along. At midday they stopped to rest again and Storm fell instantly asleep, without even taking the guitar off her shoulders.

She came awake suddenly and found herself being picked up in Luke's arms. She gave an involuntary cry and tried to jerk herself free, but he said urgently, 'Quiet. Someone's coming,' and ran with her to a patch of deep scrub among the trees. Setting her down he said, 'Stay here. Don't move,' then ran back to where they'd been resting to pick up the holdall and her guitar.

Storm could hear it now, the sound of an engine snarling its way up the track along the way they'd come. Luke slid down beside her, his body almost covering hers as they huddled in their fragile shelter. 'Can you see?' she whispered as the sound came nearer. 'It might be friends?'

'Perhaps. Keep down. Yes, I see it. It's one of the trucks from the site. Damn, I thought I'd sabotaged them all!' He brought his head down, but Storm felt him take the gun from his belt. Then they lay there as the truck's engine came closer and closer and Storm just prayed for it not to stop, to just keep going. It seemed to take an eternity and she was sure that the men on it must see where they had flattened the grass. It slowed, and her heart froze, but it was only to change gear and then the truck went on and passed them.

Only when they could no longer hear the engine did Luke move. 'Stay here,' he said in her ear. 'I'm going to make sure they're not trying to trick us.'

It was ten minutes before he came back and Storm had given him up for dead a hundred times. 'Is it all right?' she asked anxiously.

'Yes, they've gone.'

'Thank goodness! I take it they weren't friendly?'

'No. I recognised a couple of them. They were the ringleaders of the trouble at the dam. I got rid of them as soon as I arrived, but they must have been hanging around, just waiting to get a riot going.' His eyes went over her. 'Are you all right?'

'Yes. I'm ready to go on now.'

Picking up the guitar, Storm went to move towards the track but Luke stopped her. 'It will be too dangerous to use the road any more. When they don't find us they'll turn round and come back, start looking more closely. We may not be able to find any cover next time.'

Storm looked at him blankly. 'So what do we do?'

'Cut through the forest. It's the only way.'

She looked nervously at the trees that seemed to stretch endlessly into the distance. 'Are you sure we won't get lost?'

'No, we'll be fine,' he assured her, shouldering the holdall, adding when he saw her anxious face, 'Trust me, Storm.'

She laughed. 'All right. But just keep any crawly things away from me!'

Luke grinned back at her. 'So now I've found your weakness, have I?'

'And some. I warn you, if I see a snake or something I'll scream my head off and you won't see me for dust.'

'Don't worry, they're far more scared of you. When they hear us coming they'll soon get out of our way.' He set off into the forest with Storm close on his heels, her eyes scanning the ground for snakes, her ears pricked for the sound of the truck returning.

It was impossible to be so tense for very long, and after half an hour or so she began to relax. They were far enough from the road now not to be seen and the undergrowth was sparse so that there was no real danger of her treading on a snake. Actually it was better walking in the forest than on the track because they had the shade of the trees and the ground wasn't so uneven. Occasionally brightly coloured birds flew out of the trees, and butterflies so beautiful that they caught at her heart winged their way through the air, the sun shining through their almost translucent bodies. Once she was startled by a monkey who ran chattering in fury away from them, making her stop and laugh as she watched him.

Luke turned and waited for her.

'Did you see him?' Storm asked delightedly. 'Wasn't he mad at us for disturbing him! I've never

seen a monkey in the wild before, only in zoos and
safari parks.' She realised that Luke wasn't really
listening, that his eyes were quite openly looking her
over. As she realised how terrible she must look with
her unbrushed hair, unmade-up face, and stained and
torn clothes, her voice hardened. 'I bet you're really
enjoying seeing me like this, aren't you? I bet it gives
you a real kick!'

'Yes,' Luke agreed, 'I am. But not for the reasons
you think. I had no time for the kind of woman you
were back at the bungalow. But now . . .' he grinned,
'given time I might even get to like you!'

'That's strange,' Storm agreed blandly. 'I had no
time for the kind of man you were back at the site
either—and you haven't changed a bit,' she added in
sarcastic triumph.

'Ouch!' Luke pretended to wince. 'Well, your
tongue is certainly as razor-sharp as ever.'

They pushed on, but the forest began to get thicker,
shutting out the light and Storm's shoulders drooped
with tiredness. The ground began to get a bit boggy
and they had to wade through a blocked stream,
Storm cringing as the mud sucked at her feet.

'We'd better get away from this stream,' Luke
muttered, and carried on for another half mile or so
till they came to a more open patch, guarded by tall
trees. 'This will do,' he said after giving Storm a keen
glance. 'We'll make camp here.'

She heaved a sigh of relief and let the guitar fall
from her shoulders as she sank down on her knees. 'I
don't think I've ever walked so far in my life! How far
do you think we've come?'

'Hard to say. But we should reach Bura by

tomorrow with any luck.'

'You'd probably have been there already if I hadn't been with you.'

'Rubbish.' He spread one of the blankets on the ground. 'Here, sit on this.' Glancing up at the rapidly dying daylight, he took two empty beer-cans from the holdall and quickly cut off the tops with a gadget on his knife. 'Shan't be long,' he told her, and started to jog back the way they'd come.

'Wait! Where are you going?' Storm called as she sat up in a panic. But Luke merely waved a hand and went on hurrying through the forest.

The next ten minutes weren't pleasant as the shadows of night gradually crept nearer. Storm knelt on the blanket and had never felt so alone and vulnerable in her life. The darkness seemed to be like a solid wall, getting so near that it would eventually crush her, and she gave a little whimper of fear. Luke must be lost, and they would never find each other again. She would be left to wander alone through this great forest until she died. 'Luke!' she called on a sudden tide of panic. 'Luke!' She got to her feet, knowing she would have to go and find him before it got completely dark.

She started off on the way he'd gone, calling his name, but the branch of a tree touched her face and she spun round in fear. When her heart began to beat again as she saw what it was, Storm went to go on, but realised that she'd lost her sense of direction. She froze for a moment but then blundered on, only able to see a few feet ahead now. Perhaps she'd better go back to where they'd left the blankets, but which way was back? 'Luke!' she called on a rising note of hysteria. 'Luke!'

Suddenly a branch was pushed out of the way and Luke was there, startling her out of what little was left of her wits. She gave a great gasp of relief and was ready to fall into his arms with joy.

But Luke said roughly, 'What the hell are you doing wandering about out here? Haven't you got any sense at all? Why didn't you stay where I left you, you stupid idiot?'

The inclination to hug him disappearing like magic, Storm retorted, 'I thought you were lost. I went to look for you.'

'Of all the damn stupid . . .' Cursing under his breath, he took her hand in a firm grasp and led her unerringly back to the clearing where they'd left the blankets. 'Now sit there,' he ordered like a sergeant-major. 'And don't you dare move.'

'You were gone for ages,' Storm said unrepentantly as she sat down. 'I was sure you were lost.'

'Don't tell me you were worried about me?' Luke carefully put the beer cans, now full of water, down on the ground.

She was about to admit that she had been worried, but his tone was so sceptical that she said instead, 'Certainly not. I just didn't want to be left here alone, that's all. For all I care you can get lost any time.'

'That figures.' He passed her one of the beer cans. 'No, don't drink it,' he said quickly as she went to put it to her mouth. 'It's for you to wash with.'

'But don't the natives drink it?'

'Yes, but they've been drinking it all their lives and are probably immune to the bacteria in it. We're not,

and I'd rather not risk it unless we absolutely have to.'
Standing up, he stripped off his shirt and poured the
contents of his can over his head, using his hands to
wash his body.

Storm washed more circumspectly, pouring some of
the water into her cupped hand to wash her face, arms
and chest, using most of it to get the black, smelly
mud off her feet. Then she tore another strip off her
skirt to clean her sandals. She glanced at Luke as she
did so and saw that he was unwinding the bandage
from his injured arm. 'How is it?' she asked.

'Maybe you can tell me. It's difficult to see myself.'

After rinsing her hands carefully in what was left of
the water, Storm knelt beside him to take a look. 'It's
still open, but it looks all right. I wish we had some
antiseptic powder or something to put on it."

Luke tore another piece from his spare shirt and
gave it to her. 'It's only a scratch, and I'm fit and
healthy. It will heal.'

'In your prime, huh?' Storm said on a husky note.
She was aware of his nearness again, of his broad, bare
chest with its dark mat of hair. Of a few drops of water
that still lay in the hollow of his shoulder blades, just
waiting to be licked away. Her fingers lingered for a
moment on his arm as she finished bandaging the
wound. She felt as if she wanted to go on touching
him, to run her hands over his tanned skin, to feel his
heat and strength under her fingertips. But instead
she turned quickly away, perturbed by her own
wantonness. 'I'm hungry. Can we eat now?'

Luke didn't answer for a moment, then said as if
he'd been thinking of something else, 'Oh. Yes, of
course.'

They shared the rest of one of the packets of biscuits and the last of the fruit and had a can of beer each, by which time it was completely dark. The forest had seemed quiet by day, with only the jarring call of the birds to break the silence, but now the quiet was almost total and felt heavy and threatening.

'We'd better try and get some sleep so that we can move on as soon as it's light,' Luke decided.

'Yes, all right.' Storm wrapped herself in the blanket and lay down. She could hardly see Luke now but was aware of him as a darker shadow as he lay down a few feet away. Her body, especially her legs, felt dog-tired, but mentally she was fully awake, thinking about Luke, wondering why it was that he attracted her so. He just wasn't her type. And yet there was something about him that drew her like a magnet—and repelled at the same time. He was so arrogant, so unfeeling. But no, that wasn't true. He wasn't insensitive. He'd understood about the dawn, how it had caught at her heart. But most of the time he was just a big, overbearing tyrant.

Well, he was certainly big. Her mind dwelt again on his broad chest and shoulders, until she brought it sharply back. Dear God, she was turning into a frustrated spinster, the way she kept drooling over Luke! So why not? The thought crept into her mind and wouldn't go away. If they were both attracted to each other, why couldn't they enjoy each other's bodies? Neither of them wanted to get emotionally involved and tomorrow, after they reached Bura, they would part and never see each other again. But for tonight? Storm caught her breath and drew herself into a tight, frustrated ball. It wasn't for her to make the first move. If Luke wanted her then it was up to him. But she hadn't given him any encouragement, quite the opposite, in fact. He probably thought that she hated his guts. Which was true in a way; at times—in fact most of the time—she did hate him. But then would come this overwhelming feeling of need and longing.

Oh, hell! Storm tried to forget about Luke, to shut him out of her mind completely, as he had obviously shut her. She tried to go to sleep, but then heard a rustling sound in the undergrowth close beside her and sat up with a jerk. 'Luke! There's something there.'

Instantly he was beside her. 'What?'

'I heard something. It's a snake, I'm sure it is.'

'Snakes don't move around at night,' he said positively.

'But there's something there, I tell you.'

'Wait.' He moved away and fumbled in the holdall, then came back with a box of matches and lit one, shielding it with his hand. The tiny flame in that great forest was one of the most comforting things Storm had ever known. Luke walked all round their little clearing and came back to her. 'There's nothing there. Even if there was it would have turned and fled after all your squawking.'

'I did not squawk!' The match went out and she immediately felt nervous again. 'I didn't know you had some matches.'

'I brought them from the bungalow.'

'Oughtn't we to light a fire—to keep the wild animals away?'

'And to show any predatory humans just where we

are?' Luke answered shortly. 'Sorry, no.'

'We're miles into this forest. Who could possibly see a little fire? Just a little one,' she coaxed.

'I said no.'

'You're a louse, Luke! I didn't get any sleep last night because I kept watch when you were hurt, and now you won't let us have even a tiny fire so that I can get some sleep tonight.'

Luke gave a snort of derision. 'Is that how you usually get your own way—by using moral blackmail?' He rolled himself in his blanket again. 'Go to sleep, Storm. Nothing will attack you—it wouldn't dare in case it got its head bitten off.'

She glared at his shadow, and tried to go to sleep again, her thoughts about him completely different now. But he was wrong; she hadn't been asleep very long before a continuous buzzing noise got through to her subconscious and became too insistent to be ignored. Sitting up, she cursed and thrashed madly at the air with her arms.

'Now what is it?' Luke demanded in a voice of long suffering.

'I'm being bitten to death by mosquitoes. Aren't they biting you?'

'They don't bother me too much any more. I suppose I've got immune to them. I'm sorry. I thought we'd moved far enough away from the stream for them not to bother us.'

'I tried to pull the blanket right over me, but then I can't breathe.'

There was a pause and then Luke moved over beside her. 'You'd better lie close to me and I'll try to protect you as much as I can.'

So they lay side by side on a blanket, the other pulled over them, and Luke put his arm round her waist, drawing her close up to his body. 'Maybe whatever they don't like about me will put them off you.'

Rather overcome at being held so near to him, Storm said flippantly, 'So you repel mosquitoes as well as everything else.'

His arms tightened round her waist. 'Watch it, woman, you're in a vulnerable position.'

And also a very frustrating one, Storm thought, and wondered if he felt it too. Was coming over here and holding her like this to be the first move? She waited tensely, but Luke didn't follow it up, and eventually she fell asleep in his arms, too tired to stay awake any longer.

A couple of times in the night she came partly awake, unused to sleeping with anyone, and Luke murmured soothingly in her ear. Reassured, Storm fell asleep again, and finally came fully awake to the sound of a bird singing its rich dawn song in a tree above her head. Opening her eyes, she looked up and saw the blue sky and sunlight filtering through the branches of the trees. She lay still, aware of Luke's arms around her but content just to listen until the bird had sung its heart out and flown away to find another tree.

'Quite an alarm clock, isn't he?' Luke murmured.

'Mm.' She turned her head to find that he was fully awake. His beard had grown in the night and left a shadow of stubble around his jaw. 'You won't be able to shave today. You'll be fashionable—designer stubble.'

'Mm.' He looked at her still drowsy face, at the long golden eyelashes on her heavy-lidded eyes, and the soft, relaxed curve of her mouth. 'I hope it doesn't scratch too much.' And he bent to kiss her.

It felt right, that kiss. Soft and warm and undemanding. He took her mouth with enjoyment, savouring its sweetness, exploring the fullness of her lower lip, and gently tasting with his tongue the warmth within. It wasn't the kiss of a lover. Even when Storm recovered from her first surprise and began to respond, Luke didn't let it deepen into passion. It was almost as if they'd spent the whole night making love and had woken in the morning, still satiated, but close and tender and companionable. And in a sudden surge of longing Storm had a brief glimpse of what life with a man like Luke could be like. Putting her arms round his neck, she closed her eyes, drowning in his kiss, wishing, pretending.

But all too soon Luke raised his head and she opened her eyes to see him smiling lazily down at her. 'That was a very nice way to start the day.' Then he gave a little grimace. 'Do you think I could have my arm back now—I'm not sure it belongs to me any more!'

Storm sat up and Luke got to his feet, rubbing the arm she'd used for a pillow all night. It was still very early, with a thin ground mist hovering among the trunks of the trees. Luke went to get water for them to wash with, and they breakfasted again on biscuits and beer.

'Careful,' he warned her when she went to take another biscuit. 'That's our last packet. And there's only one more can of beer.'

'But we'll reach Bura today, won't we?'

'Should do. I reckon the main road isn't far from here. Once we reach that we'll only have about twenty miles to go.'

'*Only* twenty!' Storm groaned, and rubbed at a mosquito bite.

'Did you get badly bitten?'

'Mostly on my hands and neck.' The mosquito bites were irritating like mad, especially where her necklace was rubbing, and with an impatient movement she took off all the jewellery she had round her neck and stuffed it in the pocket of her shirt. Her hands, too, had been bitten, so she also took off her rings. 'The rest of me isn't too bad. Thanks to you.' She looked into his face, remembering the closeness of the night and the way he'd kissed her, wondering if it had meant anything to him. But if it had he certainly didn't show it. He seemed in a hurry to move on and within twenty minutes of waking they were on their way again.

The mist soon cleared and the trees thinned again, birds rising into the air from the branches as they passed and giving out cries of annoyance at being disturbed. They found a wild banana plant and picked some of the fruit, plantains Luke called them, and put them in the holdall to eat for lunch. After about an hour Luke paused and held up a hand. 'We should be almost at the road. Keep your eyes and ears open.' And in another half-mile they came to it, a long ribbon of potholded tarmac that cut through the forest.

'Stay here,' he ordered. 'I'll scout ahead. I want to see whereabouts we've come out on to it.'

He dropped the holdall beside her and Storm sat down in the shade of a convenient bush, glad to rest her legs. She gave a sigh and looked longingly at the holdall, wishing she could have a drink. She was so thirsty and her stomach was rumbling with hunger. Of course, the plantains! She got to her knees and leaned over to reach for the bag—then froze as she saw a man standing behind a tree only a few yards away.

He was a native, dressed only in a shirt and sarong, his feet bare. But across his shoulders was slung a rifle and he wore a wicked-looking knife at his waist. He wasn't looking in her direction but towards the road where Luke had gone. Perhaps he hadn't yet seen her, sitting in the shade of the bush. Hardly daring to breathe, Stormed moved stealthily backwards on her hands and knees, until she was no longer in the man's sight, then started to get slowly to her feet with a wild idea of trying to get to the road to warn Luke. But as she began to rise a hand came down on her shoulder, pushing her back, and another hand came in front of her face holding a dagger with a wavy edge, its razor-sharp blade pointing towards her throat.

The hand was brown, the nails broken and dirty, but that was all Storm could see of her captor. His fingers bit into her shoulder as he forced her to her knees, and the sun caught the bright blade of his dagger as he brought it even nearer to her throat. Storm jerked her head back and saw two more men come forward and look at her. They moved quietly and kept glancing towards the road, and she knew that they were looking for Luke, waiting for him to come back. And then they would kill them both, she was

sure of it. She stiffened, realising that she had to warn
him, but her captor must have guessed her thoughts
and put the blade up to her throat so that she could
feel it against her skin.

She began to tremble, but saw the other men move
back amongst the trees out of sight, and knew that
Luke was coming. Her captor's grasp tightened
sharply and she almost cried out, but the knife bit into
her skin, drawing blood, and she knew that if she tried
to scream, she would be dead before she'd even drawn
in her breath. So Luke walked towards them,
completely unaware of the trap set for him, and there
was nothing she could do about it. Nothing.

He pushed a branch aside, saw them, and the next
second his gun was in his hand. 'Let her go or I'll kill
you,' he said savagely, and repeated it in a language
Storm didn't understand.

But the man behind her just laughed and put
his hand in her hair, jerked her head back to expose
the long, vulnerable column of her throat, a trickle
of blood already flowing down. Time seemed to
stand still as Storm looked into Luke's eyes and saw
him weighing up the chances of killing the man before
he could kill her. But in those seconds two of the
other natives came up behind Luke, the clink of their
rifles telling him of the trap. His face hardening, he
slowly extended his arm and dropped the gun on the
ground.

The next few moments were the most terrible that
Storm had ever known as she waited for them both to
be killed. But the man behind her gave an order and
one of the natives ran forward to pick up the gun,
holding it on Luke as his arms were forced up behind

his back and tied tightly. Then she too was dragged to
her feet and her hands tied, her captors looking her
over with interest and obviously making comments
about her in their own language as they did so. They
pushed her over towards Luke and she stumbled,
almost falling against him.

'Are you all right? Did he cut you badly?'

'No. Oh, Luke!' She looked at him with terrified
eyes and stood close to him, would have given
anything to feel his arms around her.

'Why didn't you scream?'

'I—I couldn't.'

He gave a snort of derision. 'The one time when it
would have helped, and you couldn't! The rest of the
time you scream like a startled hyena.'

'These *are* slightly unusual circumstances,' Storm
retorted, stung from terror to anger, as Luke had
intended. 'Why don't you talk to them or something?
Tell them who we are.'

'Quiet. They might speak English,' he said softly,
then raising his voice, he spoke again in the strange
language, addressing the man who had held her, who
appeared to be the leader of the group.

The man understood Luke and answered him
curtly, obviously enjoying his triumph.

'What did he say?' asked Storm.

'I asked him why he'd captured us and what he was
going to do with us. He said he's going to take us back
to the dam. That he knows who I am and that he'll get
well paid if he does.'

'All that way!' Storm's heart sank just at the
thought of having to walk back all those miles. What
would happen when they got there she didn't dare to

even contemplate.

Two of the men picked up their belongings and then prodded them with their rifles until they got into line and began the long trek back to the dam and whatever fate awaited them there.

CHAPTER SIX

THEIR captors were used to the forest and moved through it swiftly, making it hard for Storm to keep up, especially with her hands tied. It was so difficult to balance. Several times she fell to her knees and the man behind either prodded at her till she got up or else yanked her to her feet. When it got to about the sixth time, Storm lost her temper. Turning on the man, she yelled at him, 'Will you stop prodding me with that damn gun? You stupid imbecile! Can't you see I can't walk properly with my hands tied? Can't you see I'm tired? I want a drink and something to eat!'

The man had taken an involuntary step backwards as Storm flared at him, cannoning into Luke, who promptly sat down on the ground.

For a few moments there was confusion, until the leader made Luke translate what she'd said. Grudgingly they were allowed to rest and were given some brackish water to drink. For this Storm's hands were untied, but she lifted the water in an old bottle first to Luke's mouth so that he could drink. 'What are we going to do?' she whispered to him. 'Luke, I'm scared. We can't let them take us back.'

'Delay them as much as you can,' he murmured back. 'Try and get them to leave your hands untied.'

So when the men were ready to move on again and

came to tie her hands, she began to cry and wail,
throwing her arms around and shouting at them
until in the end she made such a fuss, refusing to get
to her feet and throwing herself down again when
they picked her up, that they left her untied just to
keep her quiet. The leader spoke sharply to Luke in
the middle of all this, but Luke shrugged eloquently
and shook his head without answering.

They set off again, the terrain becoming more hilly
as the long afternoon wore on. Storm had a great
many bruises from where she'd been prodded with the
rifle and collected more when she tripped and fell
several feet back down a rocky hillside. She lay there,
too stunned and exhausted to move, but one of the
men pulled her back to her feet and made her go on.
As she passed Luke she glanced wearily at him and
was startled to see the fury in his eyes. All afternoon
she had been walking as slowly as she dared, but now
there was no pretence, she could hardly stand. At last
the men stopped and made camp on a rocky shelf of
ground half-way up a hill. Sinking gratefully to the
ground, Storm just lay there for a long time, too spent
to move.

One of the men brought her some water and she
drank thirstily. He touched her hair admiringly, but
she jerked her head away and glared at him. Luke was
sitting down against a tree trunk, his eyes closed and
his hands still tied. He looked defeated and beaten.
He's given up, Storm thought in despair. We're
finished. Crawling over to him, she held the bottle of
water to his lips. 'Luke. Are you all right?' she asked
anxiously.

He opened his eyes a little—and winked at her.

'Come nearer,' he whispered.

Putting one arm around his neck as if to raise his head for him to drink, Storm effectively shielded him with her body and heard him say softly, 'My hands are coming looser. See if you can keep their attention off me for a while. But when I should get ready to run.'

Lifting a finger to wipe a trickle of water from his mouth, Storm looked into his eyes and saw the gleam of vibrant life and strength. Defeat and tiredness slipped from her like a winter coat in the sun and her face shone with excitement. 'I could kiss you,' she whispered.

He raised an eyebrow. 'So why don't you?'

Laughter came into her blue eyes. 'Here? Now?' But then she leant forward and put her lips against the hard dryness of his.

One of the men pulled her roughly away and made her sit several feet from Luke. Storm snapped at him, confident now that they were worth more of the men alive than dead. But the leader had had enough of her and hit her across the face, silencing her. Turning to Luke, the man spoke to him asking a question. Luke replied briefly, and the leader made a remark which the other three thought was extremely funny.

'What did you say?' demanded Storm when the men had all sat down again.

'He asked me who you were—and I told him you were my woman.'

'What—what did he say to that?'

Luke glanced at the men and saw that they weren't watching, then grinned. 'They wanted to know what use I had for a woman who shrieked like a macaw and was as scrawny as the legs of a flamingo.'

Storm's eyes widened indignantly and she glowered at him as she realised that he had much enjoyed repeating that remark. She wished now that she hadn't kissed him. But no, she didn't wish that at all. In fact . . . Her imagination wandered as she dwelt on what it might have been like if she could have gone on kissing Luke, and perhaps more, as he sat there with his hands tied, unable to do anything about it.

Her thoughts came guiltily back to reality as she remembered that she was supposed to distract their captors. How on earth did Luke expect her to do that? she wondered. The leader had opened the holdall and was going through its contents, tossing her a couple of plantains as he did so. Storm ate them ravenously, watching for an opportunity, trying to ignore Luke's surreptitious movements as he worked to get his hands free. The men divided up Luke's belongings between them, the leader getting the biggest share, and he took the first swig of the whisky when they found the bottle. That, and the last can of beer, they passed round while they ate some food they'd brought with them. Perhaps they weren't used to anything as potent as whisky, it seemed to go to their heads very quickly. Soon they were laughing drunkenly, the sort of laugh men have when they swop rude stories. They seemed to be looking round at Storm more often and were obviously talking about her. She grew uneasy but closed her eyes, pretending to be asleep, hoping that Luke would soon get his hands free, for it seemed that her just being there was distraction enough.

One of the men got up and came over to her, caught hold of her and lifted her to her feet. She tried to

fight him off, suddenly terribly afraid, but he dragged
her over to the other men and made her sit down with
them, next to the leader. He put the whisky bottle in
her hands and motioned her to drink. Storm shook her
head, but he reached angrily out to force her, so she
hastily took a sip and passed it on. The leader began to
paw her, stroking her hair which obviously fascinated
him, and her bare arm, putting his hand on her leg.
Storm swore at him and tried to move away, but that
brought her up against the man on her other side.

She began to despair, seeing the avaricious gleam in
the leader's eyes, and knowing that once he had raped
her he would pass her on to the others, just as he had
the whisky, and with as little concern. Luke's face,
when she glanced across at him, was hard and set, his
shoulders tense, and she knew that he was using all his
strength to get free. But could he do so in time? And
even if he did how could he hope to beat four armed
men and rescue her? All he could realistically hope for
was to slip away and save himself in the hope that he
could get help and come back in time to save her life,
even if he couldn't save her from anything else. Their
eyes met and she tried to tell him this, tried to convey
the unspoken message with her eyes. He understood,
she was sure of it, but he gave a very definite negative
shake of the head and winked at her again.

The leader put his hand on her breast and she
turned to shout at him, but now the men only
laughed, enjoying making her angry because they
knew she was at their mercy—or lack of it. One of
them picked up her guitar and tried to play it, which
made her so cross that she leaned across and snatched
it from him. 'Don't you dare touch that! *This* is the

way you play it.' And she played the first few bars of a
melody. The result was a gratifying surprise. The
men all stared at her and exclaimed, and the leader
motioned her to go on as soon as she paused. A
glimmer of hope ran through her and she began to
play again and then to sing, putting more into that
performance than she would have done a special
concert in London or New York. While she could
keep the men entertained it would keep their minds
off her as a woman and most definitely off Luke.

She sang until she became hoarse and the whisky
bottle was empty, one man having fallen into a
drunken sleep where he sat and another looking as if
he could hardly stay awake a moment longer. Her
throat parched, Storm had to stop and point at the
bottle of water. The leader gave it to her, but started
to touch her as soon as she picked it up to drink. She
knew that she couldn't hold him off any longer. She
had given Luke—and herself—all the time she could,
but Luke was still sitting with his hands behind his
back. There was only one chance left. Holding the
neck of the bottle in her hands, Storm shifted her grip
so that she could use the bottle as a weapon.
Summoning up all her courage, she started to swing it
at her tormentor, but just then Luke gave a shout and
the man turned away so that the bottle only gave him
a glancing blow. But it gave Luke enough time to
launch himself at the other man and knock him down,
grabbing for his gun with arms that were still numb
from being tied so long.

But the leader wasn't going to lose his chance of a
rich reward. He snatched the bottle and threw it away,
then pulled Luke's own gun from his belt, fumbling

with the unfamiliar safety catch. But he had forgotten Storm. While he snarled at Luke to keep back, she caught up the guitar and swung it in both hands like a giant club. It caught the leader on the side of the head and knocked him down, the gun flying from his hand.

'Quick, get the gun,' Luke ordered, and Storm ran to pick it up while Luke found enough strength in his wrists to knock the other man out. The third native had staggered to his feet, reaching for a knife, but when he saw two guns trained on him he changed his mind and raised his hands high in the air. The fourth man slept happily through the whole thing.

Luke used the rope that had bound them to tie the men up, then took their rifles and swung them against a tree until they broke in pieces. Their knives he took from them and put in the holdall, except for one which he carried to the edge of the hillside and threw down into the forest below. 'Why did you do that?' Storm wanted to know.

'Just in case we can't send anyone back to pick them up for a few days. They should be able to get down the hill and given time will find the knife and be able to cut themselves free. But not until we've got well clear.' Without compunction he took the rest of the men's food, but left them the water bottle. The leader started to swear and curse at them, but Luke strode over and pulled him to his feet. 'You,' he said viciously, 'are going to be taught some manners. And the first thing is that you don't hit women.' And he hit the man hard in the face, just as he had hit Storm.

Picking up her battered guitar, Storm turned and walked away, heard the leader give a groaning cry as

Luke hit him again, then silence, as Luke came to join her.

'Thanks,' she said huskily as he walked up to her.

He laughed. 'I'm glad you're not squeamish! And thanks for knocking him down, by the way. My arms had been bent behind me so long I could hardly move them.'

'He deserved it, putting his filthy hands on me. God, I'd give anything for a bath! He's made me feel dirty.'

Luke put his arm round her shoulders and looked at her in the bright moonlight. 'You've never looked more beautiful,' he said sincerely, and gave her one hard kiss on the mouth before laughing down at her. 'Come on. We'd better get away from here before anyone else shows up.'

They walked for a couple of hours through the cool night forest, until Storm was too tired to go on, then she slept with her head in Luke's lap while he kept watch through the rest of the night.

The next morning they pushed on almost as soon as she awoke, eating what was left of the food, but troubled by thirst until Luke found a coconut freshly dropped from a palm tree and managed to open it with one of the natives' knives.

'Mm, delicious,' Storm said gratefully as she drank the milk and bit into a piece of the flesh that he handed to her. 'Where do you think we are?'

Looking up at the sun, Luke grimaced. 'A good ten miles or so from where we were yesterday, I think. It's hard to say in the forest, but if we keep going north we must either reach the main road or the coast.'

'The coast?' Storm repeated, brightening. 'We

could have a swim.' She ate some more and said, 'One thing I don't understand. When we were back at the dam and you talked to the workers that time, you used an interpreter. But you talked to those men who captured us in their own language. Why was that?'

'The men at the mine were mostly from this island and spoke a dialect I don't understand, but those four men must be from one of the other islands and spoke the official language of Indonesia, which is close to Malay.'

'Did they work at the mine?'

Luke shook his head. 'I didn't recognise them. Presumably they were out to stop people travelling on the main road, which is rather worrying. If there's one gang there may be more. It may mean that we'll have to stick to the forest and open country as much as we can.'

Storm gave a little laugh. 'When I think of all the limos that Wayne always had waiting for us wherever we went! I'll never take one for granted again.'

'Who's Wayne?' he asked.

'Oh—he's my manager. Wayne Forrester.'

'Has he been with you long?'

'Mm, quite some time. Almost since I started.'

Luke waited for her to go on, but she didn't, and he got to his feet. 'Let's get going. We'll save the rest of the coconut for later.'

They walked on for several hours, Luke in front but swaying a little from tiredness, his eyes going up to the sun to continually check their position. Storm followed ten yards or so behind him, doggedly trailing him and determined not to ask for a rest. The forest had become familiar now and held no fears for her;

she knew that any noise she heard in the undergrowth was of wild things running *away* from them. But the birds and the butterflies had become familiar too, and she took their beauty for granted. The weather had changed a little today, becoming overpoweringly hot until the heat was broken by a thunderously heavy tropical rainstorm. Storm had welcomed it at first, standing out in it like a shower and letting the rain cleanse her hair and body and clothes, laughing with pleasure at being clean again.

But the rain hadn't stopped for over half an hour and their blankets were so soaking wet that they had to abandon them. It made walking harder afterwards too, so that they went much slower. But the forest seemed to come alive, the earth giving off a rich, verdant smell that filled their nostrils, the trees dripping an orchestration of raindrops on to the broad-leafed undergrowth, which steamed in the heat. For a while Storm enjoyed the change, even though it was so much more difficult to walk, but it teemed down twice more and took the fun element away.

It was when Luke was thinking of making camp, about four in the afternoon, that disaster hit them again. He stepped into what looked to his tired, aching eyes to be an ordinary clearing and found himself sinking into the oozing mud of a deep swamp.

He gave a cry of alarm and Storm looked up to see him already up to his waist. She shouted, 'Luke!' and ran towards him to help.

'Get back!' Luke floundered in the mud, trying to turn, but as he did so the mud pulled him deeper as if it was a hungry, living thing.

'Try to lie flat,' Storm shouted, and edged cautiously forward, trying to get as near to him as possible.

With a supreme effort Luke managed to turn round and lean forward as much as he could, but his body was already so deep that he couldn't get his legs up. 'Try and find a branch!' he shouted, his voice still calm even though death was only a few horrendous inches away.

Looking round desperately, Storm saw a log and ran to pick it up, but it disintengrated in her hands, huge insects crawling away from the nests they had made in its rotten interior. There was nothing else, nothing that would do. She ran wildly back and became aware of the guitar bumping against her back. With a sob, she pulled the strap over her head and lay on the grass, holding one end of the guitar tightly and extending the other to Luke. But the mud seemed to have pulled him farther away, and she had to edge out on to it herself before he could reach.

The mud was up to his shoulders now, but he could still raise his hands to grab the guitar and wind the strap round his wrist. 'OK—pull!'

Storm eased backwards, the foetid smell of the bubbling mud so foul that it made her want to vomit. She felt it plucking at her knees and feet like hands trying to draw her in, and she had to fight overwhelming terror and the almost desperate need to get back on the grass and be safe. Stubbornly she hung on to the guitar, exerting all her strength to pull Luke out, but although she strained until her arms felt as if they were coming out of their sockets, he didn't seem to be moving at all. 'Luke, I can't. It isn't any good,' she cried in despair.

'Easy. Rest a minute.' Luke's face was almost covered with mud, only his eyes, still strong and fighting, were clear. Storm took great comfort from them and from the fact that he hadn't sunk any deeper. But if she couldn't pull him out they couldn't just lie there for ever, fighting the mud. Sooner or later one of them was going to give up and go under. 'Listen. Do you think you can just hold on to the guitar while I try and heave myself out?'

'Yes.' Storm spat out some mud that tasted like rotten meat and nodded.

'Good girl. But I want you to promise me something first. If you feel yourself starting to sink you must let go and get back on firm ground. Do you understand?'

'Oh, Luke,' Storm said wretchedly.

'You've got to promise, Storm, or I'm going to let go right now.'

'*No*! All—all right, I promise.'

'Right. Tell me when you're rested and ready.'

Storm waited a few minutes for her heart to stop thumping and her aching muscles to stop burning, but she could imagine how it must be for Luke, trapped there in the stinking mud, and she soon nodded. 'I'm—I'm ready.'

'Fine. Now all you have to do is to hang on to the guitar. And don't forget to back off if you feel yourself sinking.'

'Yes. Luke . . .' Suddenly there was so much she wanted to say and no words to say it with.

'I know.' Suddenly he grinned. 'But you pick the darnedest times! Now hold on.'

It took an eternity, that struggle in the mud. Storm fought to keep it out of her mouth and nostrils, turning her head to breathe as Luke's weight on the guitar threatened always to pull her down with him. She spread her legs wide, struggling to keep her body flat, to swim on the surface as she knew she must. Her arms holding the guitar felt as if they were being torn from her body as Luke slowly inched himself out, each centimetre gained a struggle of fierce determination.

Several times they had to rest, Luke already weakened from his wound and from lack of proper food, but gradually his shoulders came out and then his chest.

Storm had given up trying to watch him, she was concentrating on keeping her face clear and holding on, just holding on although her body ached with almost unbearable pain. Then she felt him touch her hand and looked up in joyful wonder. 'Luke!' She called his name and got a mouthful of mud but didn't care. Clasping his wrist, she somehow found further resources of strength and began to move slowly backwards on to firm ground, pulling him with her.

He came quickly now, his hips, his knees and then his feet coming free with a loud slurping noise, and he was able to crawl forward until he too was on firm ground. Storm grabbed him as he came, holding him tightly as if the mud might yet take him back, tears of relief and happiness tracing trails down her mud-caked face. 'Oh, Luke, Luke!'

'It's all right.' Putting up a hand, he touched the tears on her cheek. 'Don't cry. It's over now, sweetheart.'

But she went on holding him as they knelt on the ground, hardly able to believe that the danger was over and they were safe. A noise from the swamp caught their attention and they turned their heads to see the guitar starting to sink, the mud bubbling around it, the pockets of air exploding loudly as if the mud was angry at losing its prey and was taking its spite out on the innocent instrument. Luke made a lunging movement to go and grab it, but Storm held him back in fear. 'No! Let it go. It isn't worth it.'

He glanced at her face, sharpened by fright, and then they both watched as the guitar that had done them such good service slipped sickeningly out of sight. Storm shuddered convulsively, realising how close it had been to Luke disappearing like that, the thick, putrid-smelling mud filling his mouth and nose and eyes as she watched him die. She clung to him again, her fingers digging into him. 'Hold me—oh God, Luke, please hold me. I thought you were going to die. I thought you were going to die!'

Her body shook with sobs as Luke held her, murmuring soothingly, his arms about her the greatest comfort she had ever known. It was some time before she had cried away her fear and lay quiet in his arms, and by then it was almost dark. 'Oughtn't we to get away from here?' she murmured.

Luke shook his head decisively. 'Too dangerous. We might hit another pocket of swamp. Better to stay here.'

'Oh, *good*,' Storm sighed with relief. 'I'm so tired. My whole body aches—as if I've been tortured on a rack.'

'Sleep then, my darling.'

They lay down on the grass, the stench of corruption in their nostrils as they lay close together, Luke's arms protectively round her. Storm fell asleep almost at once, too exhausted to care any more about the filth coating her clothes and body, but Luke lay awake for some time, staring up at the stars, until he too fell into a deep sleep.

They slept late, too used to the noises of the forest by now to be disturbed by them, the sun already quite high in the sky when Luke at last sat up with a groan, his limbs aching. His movements wakened Storm, she stirred and yawned, went to rub her eyes and found that her face was covered in dried mud. She sat up, staring owlishly at Luke. He looked like one of those primitive tribesmen who cover themselves completely in thick mud to take part in their religious ceremonies. Every inch of him was covered in the beastly stuff. Luke looked back and the mud at the sides of his mouth cracked as he grinned. 'You don't look as if you're exactly ready for a Royal Command Performance yourself!'

Storm continued to stare at him for a moment and suddenly they were both laughing uproariously, their mirth rippling through the forest and frightening the birds and animals away.

'If only you could see yourself!' Storm gasped. 'You look terrible, really frightening.'

'Yeah?' He pretended to leer at her. 'Ever been kissed by a mud man?'

'No!' Storm shrieked, but her attempts to fight him off were half-hearted to say the least, and Luke soon grabbed her and pulled her to him. But as his head

drew close to hers, the laughter left his eyes and they
grew dark. 'You know something,' he said huskily.
'I'm crazy about you.'

He kissed her then, the mud tasting on their lips
and tongues, but it was a kiss of deep tenderness and
meaning for all that, leaving them both emotionally
shaken when at last he let her go.

Smiling mistily up into his eyes, Storm said, 'Luke
Ballinger, I may never forgive you for this.'

'Forgive me?' he said in surprise. 'For what?'

'For telling me that—that you care about me when I
look like this.'

He laughed. 'You get more beautiful with each layer
of dirt. And I not only care about you—I'm in love
with you.' Smiling, he put a hand on her shoulder.
'When we get out of this . . .'

'If we ever do.'

'*When* we get out of this,' he repeated firmly, 'I'm
going to show you just how much I love you. But
right now, I think we ought to get going, and we'd
better take it slowly until we get out of this swampy
area.' He looked round. 'What happened to the
holdall?'

They searched and found it where Luke had flung
it off when he'd first started to sink in the swamp. So
at least Luke had a knife to defend them with,
although the gun was lost in the mud. They had
nothing to eat or drink either, and Storm felt as if she
would have given every piece of jewellery in her
pockets just for some clean, cold water to wash the
foul mud from her mouth. Moving very cautiously,
they circled the swampy area, making a big detour
until they were back in the right direction again and

could travel more quickly. Once free of the swamp their luck seemed to improve, for they found some plantains and another coconut which they ate ravenously.

The ground became hilly again, which made walking more difficult, but when they climbed to the top of a steepish hill and paused to rest, Luke said, 'Look,' and pointed across a distant valley.

'What is it? I can't see . . . Oh!' Storm exclaimed in delight. 'A village. Oh, thank heavens! We'll be able to get some help. Maybe even a car.'

'Or maybe not,' Luke said evenly.

She turned to look at him pleadingly.

'Can't we try? They might be friendly. The whole rebellion might be over by now.'

'It wasn't over yesterday when those men caught us,' Luke reminded her grimly.

'They might not have known.'

'Possibly. But somehow those kind of men always know which side to be on. If the authorities had regained control they would have been helping us, to try and get a reward, instead of taking us to be held as hostages.'

'But the people in that village might not be part of the rebellion,' Storm persisted. 'Please, Luke, can't we try?'

He shook his head decisively. 'We daren't risk it, sweetheart, I'm sorry.'

She was silent a moment, biting her lip to fight back words of anger and appeal. At length she said, 'If it wasn't for me—would you risk going to the village to find out?'

'I don't know. Trouble with being a European in an

Eastern country, you stand out as a foreigner and there's no way you can disguise yourself.' He grinned. 'Even with this mud all over us we're still too tall to be taken for natives. So I think we'd better just . . .'

His voice died as Storm turned abruptly away and began to stride down the other side of the hill, her shoulders tense. Luke went quickly after her and caught her wrist to bring her to a halt as soon as he came up to her. Putting his hands on either side of her face, he said earnestly, 'I know what you're thinking and it's all true. I am a louse and a fool for getting you into this. I know it's no place for you and you should never have got mixed up in it. You're probably right that the village is friendly and we're only a couple of hours' walk away from help. But I don't dare let you take that risk, Storm, especially not now.' His thumb caressed her mud-stained cheek. 'My darling, you've been unbelievably brave and strong. Please don't crack up on me now. Please be patient until we reach Bura and can get to safety. Because getting you safely back means so much to me now.'

'Oh, Luke!' Reaching up, she took his hand in both hers and held it very tightly. Then she smiled and kept her hand in his as they began walking on together.

The forest quite quickly gave way to cultivated areas of rubber trees and rice paddies, which they carefully skirted. Once they saw some women working in a paddy field, their backs bent as they worked knee-high in water. Storm paused for only a moment to watch them, but without making any comment turned to follow Luke again.

Leaving the village behind, they had to traverse a range of hills, but Luke encouraged Storm by telling her he thought this was the last range before they reached the big plain that surrounded the more settled area around Bura. It was hot now and they were both troubled by thirst, the mud caking hard on their bodies and giving off a most unpleasant odour. They paused to rest in the shade of a tree and Storm lifted her head. 'Listen. Do you hear it?'

'What?' Luke looked round the sky expecting to see a plane.

'No. It sounds like water.' Her eyes lit up. 'Oh, Luke—*water*!'

'Come on.' Taking her hand, Luke followed his ears, gradually increasing his pace until they were both running through the trees, pushing the undergrowth aside carelessly in their haste. They burst through the outspreading boughs of a frangipani and then both came to a sudden stop, Storm crying out in delight at what she saw. Ahead of them, in the dappled shade of exotic flowering shrubs, was a pool and above it, flowing over rocks that jutted out from the hillside, a tumbling cascade of water that sparkled like diamonds in the sunlight.

'Oh, how wonderful!' Without hesitation, she ran to the side of the pool and jumped into it, clothes, shoes and all. It only came up to her knees, but she promptly sat down, laughing and splashing the water over herself. 'Oh, God, it's beautiful, beautiful, beautiful!'

Luke had walked round the pool, making sure that all was safe, but now he came to the edge and stood grinning down at her for a minute, enjoying her happiness, before he dropped the holdall, took off his boots and came to join her in the pool.

For several minutes they were happy to just play in it, delighting in its coolness and freshness, going to the waterfall to drink and to stand up underneath it to wash their hair and faces. Taking the jewellery from her pockets, Storm put it on the bank and began to try to wash her clothes while she still wore them. But Luke came over to her and caught her hands. 'Don't be silly,' he said huskily. 'Take them off.'

She gazed into his eyes for a long moment, then let her hands fall. Reaching for the buttons on her shirt, Luke slowly began to undo them, his eyes intent. When the last button was undone he pushed the material aside and slipped the shirt off her shoulders. She wasn't wearing a bra and her nipples had already hardened from the coolness of the water. His face sharpening with desire. Luke used his hands to scoop up more water and wash away the caked mud, his touch infinitely gentle. It took him quite a time and his hands grew bolder as he worked. Storm sighed and moved against him, wanting to be held close to him but savouring each second, each touch, knowing that it would never be quite as wonderful and exciting as this ever again. When her top half was clean to his satisfaction, he took off her skirt and then her panties, letting them just float to the edge of the pool.

When he bent to wash her now she trembled and gripped his shoulders, her mouth opening on a gasping sigh of sensuality. She gazed down at him, her body aching as his hands cleansed and stroked her legs, her thighs. 'Luke.' She said his name on a wild plea of longing, and pulled him up beside her. They kissed in a sudden frenzy of desire, Storm's hands tearing at his shirt that was already ragged. She felt his skin against her own and moaned as she held him close, but yearning to be closer still. Luke kicked off the rest of his clothes and drew her under the waterfall, letting the water cascade off them as they kissed in a wild fever of passion, their desire too strong now for gentleness.

Lowering his head, he kissed her breasts, delighting in their youth and firmness, drinking the water that ran down them as he sucked and kissed her nipples. To Storm's love-starved body it was the most sensuous thing she had ever known. She moaned and pressed her hips against his, feeling the mat of hairs against her stomach, his body as aroused as hers.

Straightening up, Luke put his hands on either side of her head, his shoulders hunching over her as he kissed her fiercely. 'I love you,' he shouted over the noise of the fall. 'I love you!'

'I know. Oh, Luke. Oh, my darling!'

'Say it. I want to hear you say it.'

There was a note of yearning in his voice that made Storm gaze up at him, knowing suddenly the power she had over him. She smiled and laughed through the tumbling water, pushing the wet hair from his face. 'Of course I love you, you big fool,' she shouted back. I've been in love with you for days, and I'm going to go on loving you till the day I die!'

With a great shout of pure happiness Luke put his hands on her waist and lifted her up high above his head, swung her round while she laughed at him. Her legs went round his waist as they kissed exuberantly, her arms round his neck.

'Oh, sweetheart,' Luke said as he carried her into the centre of the pool. 'I'm crazy about you. Making love to you is going to be the most wonderful moment of my life.'

Storm's hands gripped him tightly, her body longing for fulfilment. 'So what the hell are you waiting for?' she demanded thickly.

Luke's eyes held hers, his face taut with desire and passion. Then his hands tightened on her waist as he lifted her again—and brought her down on the hard thrust of his manhood. Storm cried out, just once, but her cry changed to a rising moan of pleasure as Luke made love to her, using his body to excite them both until their groans of shared ecstasy echoed through the trees, as wild and primitive as the forest itself.

CHAPTER SEVEN

THEY lay half in and half out of the pool in a patch of sunlight. Sated with love, they were content to lie very close, to kiss lightly and to touch each other caressingly, still filled with the wonder of knowing each other's bodies and finding transcendent sexual fulfilment therein.

'We ought not to stay here much longer,' Luke warned.

Using her fingertips to draw patterns in the wet hair on his chest, Storm said dreamily, 'I don't ever want to leave. I want to stay here and have you make love to me for ever.'

He grinned and kissed her eyes, his beard grown longer now. 'I said I was going to wait until we were safe before I showed you how much I love you, but I guess I got carried away.'

'What more romantic place than this?' She looked around her at the clearing, at the diamond-studded waterfall tumbling over the rocks, at the flowering shrubs, heavy with scented blossom. 'I shall always remember this place. Always. And I'm glad it was here and not some hotel bedroom.' She smiled and lifted her head to kiss him. 'Somehow we seem to belong here now.'

Luke kissed her in return, exploring her mouth, delighting in their easy intimacy. But presently he drew back. 'Watch it, woman, or I may get carried away again!'

Storm's eyebrows rose incredulously. '*Again?*'

Luke laughed warmly. 'It's been a long time.' His eyes softened. 'I hope I didn't hurt you.'

'I can take it.' And she looked at him with a new contentment in her eyes.

'And return it with interest.'

She smiled. 'I wanted you too.'

'So I noticed,' he said smugly, and laughed when she hit him playfully. But then his face grew serious. 'This manager of yours; has there been anything between you?'

Storm hesitated for a moment, then said, 'He asked me to marry him, and I—I nearly said yes. It would have been so easy to say yes. I was tired, and he kept pressuring me. But I knew I wasn't in love with him.' She paused, her hand involuntarily tightening on Luke's arm. 'I'd been working so hard. I felt that if I didn't get away I'd crack up,' she went on. 'That's why I came here. I told Wayne that I wanted time to think it over, but it was really to try and get away from the nightmares I kept having.'

'Nightmares?'

'Yes. I kept dreaming that I was on the stage singing, but all the people in the audience gradually became just heads with huge mouths and teeth, waiting to—to tear me to pieces if I didn't please them.' She shuddered, feeling again the terror that had awoken her on so many nights.

'But you didn't tell him about them?'

'No.' She shook her head.

'Then thanks for telling me,' murmured Luke,

kissing her forehead. 'Do you still get them?'

'Two or three times when I first came to Taruna, that's all. It didn't even come back last night.'

'Good.' Picking her up in his arms, Luke carried her out of the pool and laid her down on a patch of grass in the full glare of the sun. 'I'll collect our clothes.'

He found them eventually, although one of her sandals had floated quite a way down the stream that led from the pool. He hung them on bushes to dry in the sun and lay down beside her on the grass.

'You'll get your white bits burnt,' Storm murmured, running her hand in possessive pleasure along his body.

'So will you,' laughed Luke. 'But you've been sunbathing topless; you only have marks down here.' And he traced his finger along the outline until she squirmed deliciously.

Storm chuckled in rich enjoyment and said, 'I wonder what Jerry and Anne would say if they could see us now.' Then a thought occurred to her and her blue eyes shadowed. 'Do you think they know what's happened here?'

'Bound to, I should think. You can't keep something like an uprising quiet for very long, even on a remote island like this.'

'I wonder if Jerry is still in Australia or whether he came back here. He was due to come back to Taruna the day after we left the dam site. Lord, how long ago that seems!' She thought back for a moment over those days, then frowned. 'Will they know that we're missing? I hope Anne isn't worrying about us.'

'If Jerry has any sense he won't have told her, even

if he knows. And I doubt that he does; there's probably a lot of confusion in Bura.'

'Do you think we'll reach there safely?'

'Of course.' He smiled at her. 'Nothing is going to stop us now.' He began to caress her, his eyes going over her slim body, her lovely face, her hair that had dried into a lion's mane of thick golden curls. 'You're like a cat,' he said thickly. 'A beautiful golden cat preening itself in the sun.'

Storm smiled, knowing that he wanted her yet again. 'A cat, huh?' She snuggled closer to him. 'Tell me, when did you first fall for me?'

Luke's mouth curled into a grin. 'I didn't actually fall for all of you at once. First it was your legs. When you hitched up your skirt to climb into my plane that very first day, and I saw those long, shapely legs of yours . . .' He smiled in happy reminiscence. 'Boy, I really fell!'

'You didn't act as if you had.'

'Probably because you were going on about being kept waiting so much. If it hadn't been for your legs I would have tossed you out of the plane.'

Deciding to ignore this, Storm began to rub her leg along Luke's and said complacently, 'What next did you fall for?'

'Your figure, of course. When I saw you in that bikini. After that I didn't sleep too well at nights.'

'So you like my body?' And she moved against him sensuously.

'You know damn well I'm crazy about your body,' he answered thickly. 'I've wanted you ever since you came to Taruna. But I'd made up my mind not to let you know it. You were so damned argumentative and mixed up. And your world was so different from mine. I decided that even if you were willing it would only be an unsatisfactory interlude for both of us. So I decided to try and steer clear of you.'

'But you didn't succeed,' she said softly.

'No, thank God. When I realised that I was in love with you . . .'

'When?' Storm broke in. 'When did you realise?'

Luke laughed. 'I think it was when I saw you hit that native bandit over the head with your guitar! I knew then that there was a hell of a lot more to you than the dressed-up doll that you appeared to be.'

'A double-edged compliment if ever I heard one!' Storm exclaimed indignantly. 'You deserve to be punished for that!'

He raised a derisive eyebrow. 'Oh, yeah. Says who?'

'I say so—and I know exactly how I'm going to do it.' Pushing him down on to his back, she looked teasingly down at him for a moment—then proceeded to show him exactly what she meant.

It was quite some time before they had breath for words again, then Luke asked raggedly, 'Why did they call you Storm?'

'I was born in the middle of a thunderstorm.'

'I can believe that,' he said sincerely. 'My God, you're wild!'

'Do you mind?'

'Mind? I loved every minute of it.'

Storm hugged him happily, but she pressed against his wound and he drew in his breath sharply. 'Oh, I'm sorry. Is it still painful?'

'It was OK yesterday, but it's starting to throb again now.'

'Let me look.' Storm with difficulty untied the strip of bandage round his arm and laid bare the wound, then gave a bitten-off exclamation of horror.

'What is it?' Luke demanded.

'Oh, Luke, I—I'm afraid it's infected. It looks terribly red and angry. And I think,' she raised unhappy eyes to meet his, 'I think it must have broken open when you were pulling yourself out of the swamp and some mud got into it.'

'So we'll just clean it again,' he said levelly. 'At least we've got plenty of fresh water to do it with.' He gave her an encouraging grin. 'Don't worry, I've had far worse than this.'

They dressed quickly and Luke held his arm under the waterfall, cleansing it as best they could and afterwards covering the wound with a fresh bandage torn from Storm's skirt.

'If that skirt gets much shorter everyone's going to see why I fell for you,' he joked.

Storm smiled but couldn't keep the anxiety out of her voice as she asked, 'How long do you think it will take us to get to Bura?'

Luke shrugged. 'Depends on how many detours round villages we have to make. If we could pick up a road and just walk straight there it might only take a few hours, but as it is . . .'

He left the sentence unfinished and they set off again after eating the last of their fruit and coconut. But food wasn't so much of a worry now, because they were near cultivated land and there were orange and lemon groves, mango and papaya trees that they could take the fruit from. Twice in that afternoon they skirted more villages, and at the second one almost got caught when a woman with a basket full of breadfruit on her head came walking through the forest towards the village. Luckily she was singing to herself in a high, almost chanting voice, and this gave them enough time to hide among some bushes until she had gone by.

'That was close,' remarked Luke. 'We'd better try and take a wider swing round the village.'

There was a heavy note in his voice and his eyes looked tired. There were tiny beads of sweat, too, on his lips and his forehead.

'I'm tired,' Storm said firmly. 'I think we ought to stay here for the night.'

'No, it's early yet, we ought to push on, get farther away from that village.' He looked at his watch. 'That can't be right. Damn, it's broken.' He got fretfully to his feet. 'Come on, let's get going.'

'No,' Storm refused obstinately. 'I want to stay here.'

Angrily Luke stepped forward and hauled her to her feet. 'Do as you're damn well told,' he said roughly. And holding on to her arm he made her go with him.

He pushed on for almost another two hours, his jaw grimly set, his shirt gradually becoming soaked with sweat. A couple of times, after he'd glanced up at the sun to make sure of their direction, he swayed dizzily but somehow managed to stagger on, his pace slowing. Only when the sun began to sink did he stop and say unsteadily, 'We'll make camp here.' He went down on his knees and went to take the holdall off his back, but found that he couldn't bend his arm. Running forward to help him, Storm slid the bag off him and then held him in her arms as she knelt beside him. 'Oh, Luke, you stubborn fool, why won't you admit you're ill?'

'It's nothing—a touch of fever. It will be gone by the morning.'

'Are you sure? Have you had it before?' she asked hopefully, thing of malaria and diseases like that that often recurred.

'Sure. Everyone gets a fever of some kind if they stay in the tropics long enough. Occupational hazard.'

He lay back against a tree trunk and closed his eyes, beads of sweat trailing into the dark growth of beard on his unshaven chin. Going to the holdall, Storm took out an orange, cut through its skin and went back to Luke. Tenderly she supported his head and squeezed the juice of the orange into his mouth.

'That was good.' He gave her a crooked grin. 'Maybe I'll even let you lead the way tomorrow. Think you can find your way by the sun?'

'I think so. I've watched you often enough.'

'And which way is it to Bura?'

'Due north—except when we're circling villages and swamps.'

He chuckled. 'Good girl! Just remember that and you'll be OK.'

'What do you mean? Luke?' She looked at him in sudden fear.

'I told you, it's nothing. Is there another orange?'

'Yes, of course.' She squeezed it for him and he almost immediately lay down and fell asleep. At first Storm thought that the best thing for him, but it wasn't a restful sleep, he tossed and turned on the hard ground, muttering to himself and sometimes crying out as he sank deeper into the grip of the fever.

Storm held his head on her lap in the hope of making him more comfortable and felt him sometimes shiver with cold and at other times his skin burn hot to the touch. At one point in the long night, when he was a little quieter, she undid the bandage round his arm and saw to her terror that his wound was more inflamed. He needed antibiotics, and quickly, or else—or else . . . Her mind balked at the thought, but she had to face it. If he didn't get medical attention quickly gangrene might set in and Luke might lose his arm, or—or even worse.

The night seemed interminable, but Storm was no longer afraid of the dark; she had a far worse enemy to deal with now. She tried to squeeze some more fruit juice into Luke's parched mouth, but he tossed his head so much that most of it was lost. 'Oh, Luke!' She tried to soothe him by talking to him and stroking his burning brow, but he threw himself about so much as the fever gripped him that she could hardly hold him. As the night wore on he became even hotter and spoke in broken sentences and muddled words. Often he said her name and seemed worried about her. 'Storm—go to Bura. Must go to Bura,' he babbled.

'Yes. Yes, we'll go tomorrow, my darling,' Storm soothed, but she knew that her words couldn't penetrate his poor, fevered brain. But once when she moved away to get him another orange he must have missed her, for he called her name angrily. 'I'm here,' she told him again, and he said forcefully, 'You damn well do as you're told!' Which would have made her laugh if she hadn't been so close to tears.

When morning came Luke lay spent and exhausted, but the fever still held him and he shook with cold, his teeth chattering. Storm squeezed the last of the fruit into his mouth and he opened his eyes and gripped her wrist with unexpected strength. 'Promise me—you'll—you'll go to Bura. Don't stay with me. Go now.'

'Yes, all right, I promise I'll go.'

He gazed at her with red-rimmed eyes, using all his willpower to fight the fever and concentrate. 'Go, then. Don't—worry about me. You—know the way. Go!'

'Yes.' She bent and kissed him on the forehead.

'Love you,' he muttered. 'Go to Bura.'

Storm nodded, picked up the holdall and left him lying on the grass.

But she had only walked a few yards before she stopped and leaned against a tree trunk, fighting back tears. Then she opened the bag, took out the sharpest of the knives and cut a notch in the trunk of the tree. Glancing up at the sun, she went on her way, heading not for Bura but for the village they had passed the afternoon before, and stopping every ten yards or so to cut another notch in a tree, leaving a clear trail to find her way back to Luke.

Even though she went as quickly as she could, it took her quite a time to walk back to the village. She paused on the outskirts, trying to decide on the best course of action. Should she just walk boldly into it or try to attract the attention of one of the people she could see working in the fields? The latter might give her a chance to run away if the person proved unfriendly but would probably take more time. The thought of Luke lying alone and ill in the forest made up her mind for her, but first she sorted through the jewellery in her pockets. Some of the pieces had disappeared, lost in the swamp presumably, but there was more than enough to pay for the help she needed—if the villagers were friendly. And if they didn't just rob and kill her. But that was a chance she had to take. Selecting a bracelet and a ring, Storm put them on and began to walk boldly forward towards the village.

Some children saw her first and ran shouting to fetch their mothers. Then the mothers joined in the noise as they called out to the men working in the fields. Storm walked on, a fixed smile on her face to show that she was friendly. It was only a small village with a single dirt street and one-storey houses with roofs made of woven banana leaves. Seeing an elderly man sitting outside one of the houses, she went up to him and gave a little bow. 'Good morning.'

The man stared at her for a moment, then he too got to his feet and did a little bow, greeting her with words she didn't understand. Storm gave a sigh of relief. So far, so good. Within minutes it seemed that everyone who lived there had gathered round them, talking and exclaiming to each other and making a lot of noise. Raising her voice, Storm called out, 'Does anyone here speak English?' But she was met only by blank looks and more excited chattering. They fell silent when she unzipped the holdall and took out one of the knives which she ceremoniously presented to the elderly man, much to the native's delight. Then she took out another knife, sat on the ground, and smoothing out the dusty earth, used its point to draw a series of pictures. First she drew a woman and pointed to herself, the villagers assuring her excitedly that they understood. Then she drew a man to symbolise Luke. Again they nodded. Then a car crashed into a tree—she somehow didn't think she could explain a bullet-hole in a radiator.

By now the villagers were enjoying themselves, crowding round her to see and calling back to others who couldn't. Next Storm drew her and Luke walking and then Luke lying down. She had to bring some acting into it here, groaning and throwing her arms round, then pointing to the picture in the dust. The natives loved it and clapped her performance. Storm bowed and smiled, but as quickly as she could did more drawings to show that she wanted some men to make a litter and go with her into the forest to find Luke.

There was a great deal of discussion then that she sat through impatiently, wanting to shout at them to hurry, hurry! Luke could have died by now or been attacked by some wild animal as he lay too ill to defend himself. Perhaps her anxiety communicated to them, for they seemed to make up their minds, and several men went off to one of the better built houses and returned proudly carrying a wooden bed! Storm stared at it in surprise for a moment, then nodded and clapped to show how pleased she was, and immediately set off towards the forest again, the men with the bed and most of the villagers following along behind her. Feeling much like the Pied Piper with his trail of children, Storm walked as quickly as she could, but everyone wanted to carry the bed and there were frequent stops as the men argued before changing over

At last they came near to where she'd left Luke, and Storm ran on ahead, petrified at what she might find. But Luke was still alive. Still in the grip of a raging fever, yes, but unharmed and still alive.

The villagers came up and an old woman looked at Luke and examined his arm, ignoring the advice being thrown at her from all directions. She wrapped his arm in some leaves before tying it up again, and gave him a drink from a bottle she carried with her before motioning the men to put him on the bed and pick him up. He was delirious again during the whole long journey back to the village, and often tried to throw himself off the bed, until in the end the men tied him on with some rope. Seeing him like that tore at Storm's heart, but there was nothing she could do except help to hold him still and smile continuous thanks and encouragement at the men who carried him.

Back in the village they put Luke in a house where the old woman lived and Storm left him in her care while she went to draw more pictures in the dust. This time she had more difficulty. She wanted to get Luke to the hospital in Bura, or at least to a doctor so that he could have some antibiotics, but how on earth was she supposed to draw all that? In the end she drew a car with Luke and herself in it and wrote Bura, hoping that someone would understand. They did, but there was much shaking of heads, sign language and voluble talking. The car they seemed to think was almost an impossibility, but Storm persevered, and managed at length to find out that there was a car in another village.

More pictures gained her a man to guide her and, after a last anxious look at Luke, she set out with the native to walk to the other village. It was a long way and the strap of her sandal broke, so that she had to tie it on, which made walking difficult, and it was well into the heat of afternoon before they reached their destination. The car she saw at once. It was a battered pick up truck with the top and sides made from woven banana leaves, and stood in splendour in its own corrugated iron car port. This village was much bigger than the last and the people not so open and friendly. It took more than two hours of hard bargaining before Storm got the use of the car and its driver, and cost her both her ring and bracelet. She cared little for that but just hoped the driver could be trusted.

Going back in the truck was quite an experience as the driver seemed to think he ought to show off his skills to her, and drove far too fast for the bumpy road. But at least they got there quickly, even if Storm did feel that she had been shaken apart at the seams. She wanted to load Luke into the truck at once and set out for Bura, but a lot of dust pictures were drawn to explain that it was too late and they would have to wait until tomorrow. Filled with disappointment and fear for Luke, Storm tried to argue with them, but there was no moving the driver. In an island where nearly everyone went on foot or bicycle, the man with a car could afford to exert his power and make his own terms.

Storm stayed by Luke's bedside again that night, dozing intermittently, the old woman on his other side, giving him frequent sips of her home brew. In the morning they carried him to the truck, and Storm gave the old woman a gold bracelet and the elderly man a ring which she indicated was a present for all the villagers, then they set off for Bura at last. She sat in the back with Luke's head on her lap, trying to shield him from the worst of the bumps, and just praying that they were going in the right direction.

It was the longest and the most uncomfortable ride Storm had ever taken, the driver sometimes taking detours along what seemed little better than forest tracks, but at length she saw more houses and the road became smoother as they went through a couple of small towns. Luke seemed to sleep most of the time, but he was still very hot, his clothes soaking wet with sweat, but Storm was grateful that he wasn't still delirious or throwing himself around. Whenever the truck stopped she gave him some water and some of the old woman's conconction that she had pressed on her. She just hoped that even if it didn't do Luke any good, it wouldn't do him any harm.

The truck drew up at last outside a white colonial-style house with a garden of flowering shrubs and fruit trees, with hardly any other houses in sight. Storm looked at it and then turned to the driver in anger. 'This isn't a hospital! It doesn't even look like a town!'

He didn't understand her, but said something and went to knock on the door of the house. It was opened by a woman—a European woman—who took in the situation at a glance and called out to someone in the house. A man, tall and heftily built, around middle-age, came to join her. He spoke to Storm, but she shook her head. 'I'm sorry, I don't understand.'

His eyebrows went up in surprise. 'You're English? I thought you were Dutch like us.'

'Yes. I'm—I'm trying to get to the hospital in Bura. I've got to find a doctor for—for my friend. He's terribly ill. I don't know why the driver brought us here.'

'Don't worry, he brought you to the right place. I'm a doctor, and Juliana—my wife here—is a nurse.'

'Oh, thank God!' But there was no time for indulgence in relief. They carried Luke into the house, and Storm was firmly shut out as the doctor examined him.

When he came out the doctor said, 'I've given him a large dose of antibiotics and the fever should go down within forty-eight hours.'

'And his arm?' she asked anxiously.

His face was non-committal. 'I don't know. It's too soon to tell,' he told her in his flat, clipped accent. He held out his hand to her. 'We haven't introduced ourselves. My name is Jan Van Hage. So, how did you get here? And why has your friend got a bullet wound? Did you have trouble with the rebels?'

'Yes. Haven't you? I thought it was only safe in Bura. But this isn't Bura, is it?'

'No, you're miles away. We're only a short way from the sea here. And no rebels would dare to harm us—we're too popular here.'

He and his wife made a fuss of her, listening to her story, giving her the use of their bathroom, hot food to eat, and a soft bed to lie on. Confident that Luke was in good hands, Storm went to bed, luxuriating in its comfort after so many days sleeping on the ground. Juliana had lent her a long white nightdress which hung very loosely on her, for Juliana was a much larger size, but that too felt strange, and she found it difficult to sleep.

After a while she gave up trying and padded downstairs to the room they'd put Luke in. Both Dr Van Hage and his wife were there talking together, but they broke off abruptly when Storm came in.

'Hello, couldn't you sleep? Come and sit by him—feel his head. You see, the antibiotics are working. He is not so hot now.'

She smiled tremulously. 'Can I stay with him for a while?'

'Of course. I am just going to bed, but Juliana will keep you company.'

He went out of the room, and Storm took Luke's hand and held it to her face.

'You love him very much, I can see,' commented Juliana, smiling.

'Yes. Although I really haven't known him very long—just a couple of weeks.'

'Sometimes it does not take long, sometimes it takes years to love someone enough to marry them. Are you going to marry Luke?'

Storm flushed and gave a little laugh. 'He hasn't asked me to yet.'

'But if he does, you will?'

She turned to look at Luke's head on the white pillow. His face looked thin, almost gaunt, but this only accentuated its strength, defining the hard clean lines of his jaw and cheekbones, the straightness of his nose and the height of his forehead. Even his beard, grown quite long and dark now, couldn't hide the hardness and determination of his face. He could, she knew, be quite ruthless, but she also knew how tender and loving he could be. He had arrogance and pride, yes, but he could be thoughtful and kind too. He was so many things, and there wasn't one of them that she didn't love. 'Yes,' she said without any trace of doubt in her voice, 'I'm going to marry him.'

While Juliana slept on a small bed in the corner of the room, Storm kept watch for a few hours, but then the nurse insisted that Storm go back to her room, and this time she slept soundly until sunlight lying across the bed woke her the next morning. Her first thought was for Luke, but there was little change, although his body felt cooler, which was a good sign.

She said goodbye to the driver, thanked him and saw him off back to his village, then there was little to do except sit by Luke and wait. Dr Van Hage sent a boy off to Bura on a bicycle to try to get a message through to the other workers from the dam, and also to sell another piece of Storm's jewellery. All day Luke lay in a semi-coma, sometimes stirring uneasily in his bed, often hot, but not burning up as he had before.

'The fever is taking its course,' the doctor told her. 'He should wake up tomorrow.'

And he did, about four o'clock in the afternoon. Storm was alone with him, the doctor and Juliana having gone to visit a village where they held a clinic every week. Luke stirred as he had often done and opened his eyes, but this time his eyes stayed open and there was awareness in them as he looked around the room. His gaze reached her where she was sitting quietly reading and he said hoarsely, 'Storm?'

The book went flying as she ran to kneel by his bed.

'You're awake? Oh, Luke, how marvellous!'

'Where are we?' he asked in a puzzled voice. 'I—I don't remember.' He tried to sit up, but then fell back. 'God, I feel as weak as a cat!'

'Don't try to move. Here, have a drink of water.' She held a glass for him and he drank thirstily. 'Don't worry,' she told him, stroking his hair back from his forehead, 'you've been ill, but you're going to be fine now. We're safe, quite safe. We're in a house belonging to a Dr Van Hage and his wife. They're very kind, and they . . .' But Luke's head lolled against her arm and he was already asleep again.

When he next woke he was able to listen when she told him where they were. But then Dr Van Hage came in to take Luke's temperature. 'So you are back with us, Mr Ballinger. And what adventures you have had!' he exclaimed, putting a thermometer into Luke's mouth so he couldn't answer. 'Storm has been telling us all about it. Blowing up explosives and being shot at, nearly drowning in the mud—and all because of those stupid men who have come from the other islands to make the natives unhappy. But don't worry; the government have sent some troops and soon it will be all over.'

'Have the government in Jakarta really sent some troops?' Storm asked him eagerly.

'So the boy I sent to Bura tells me. But it might just be a rumour. There is no electricity on this island, no telephones. Oh, by the way, he sold your necklace.' He handed Storm what looked like a small fortune in dirty banknotes. 'Four hundred thousand rupiah. You are a rich woman.'

'Good heavens, all that!' she exclaimed.

'It is not so much as you think. There are hundreds of rupiahs to your British pound.'

'Never mind, at least I'll be able to buy myself some new clothes.' She heard a noise and looked down to see Luke laughing as he held the thermometer in his mouth. The doctor took it out, read it and nodded.

'Now I know I'm back in the land of the living,' said Luke, still laughing weakly.

'And why shouldn't I have some new clothes? Do you want me to go around in rags?' Storm demanded.

Luke's eyes settled on her face. 'You look fine to me,' he told her tenderly.

'Oh, Luke, I'm so glad you're better. So glad.' Kneeling down beside him, she took his hand and held it tightly. 'I've been so worried about you. Promise me you'll never get ill again—I couldn't bear it!'

The doctor looked at Storm as she held Luke's hand. He frowned a little, but tactfully left the room so that they were alone.

As soon as he'd gone, Storm leaned forward and kissed Luke, then smiled at him mistily as she stroked his face. 'I'll have to shave your beard off tomorrow, it isn't fashionable any more.'

'How long have we been here?' he asked.

'A couple of days. But you were ill for two days before that when I was trying to get you here.'

'Are we in Bura? Are the other men from the dam safe?'

'No, we're somewhere near the sea. The driver I hired wouldn't take us into town. But it's quite safe here. We sent a boy to try and find out about the men, but Dr Van Hage didn't mention them, so presumably the boy couldn't find out. But don't worry about them, my darling, just concentrate on getting well. Can I get you a drink or anything?'

'Juice. Orange juice, please.' She held the glass for him and he said, 'You squeezed one before—I remember.' He lay still, trying to think, then said, 'Tell me how you got me here.'

So she described the two days of journeying, making light of it, making it sound funny, but it didn't deceive Luke. 'So now I owe you my life again,' he said huskily. 'How can I ever repay that?'

'Don't be silly,' she answered sharply. 'Owing doesn't come into it. Don't ever say it again. It just happened that way, that's all.'

He gave a crooked grin. 'One thing I do owe you, though—that's a new guitar.'

'No.' Storm shook her head. 'That one was irreplaceable.'

'I'll find a way—somehow,' he vowed.

There was a knock on the door and Juliana came in to be introduced. She brought with her some broth for Luke and afterwards sent Storm away while she helped Luke to wash. He slept then but woke again in the middle of the night, the slight groan he gave waking Storm, who was dozing in the other bed.

'Are you all right?' she asked, going anxiously to him.

'Fine. Must have lain on my arm.'

'I've got some more broth for you. Here, I'll help you.'

But he heaved himself up and took the spoon from

her. 'If you put the tray on my lap I can manage.' He ate the soup dutifully but distastefully. 'When can I have some proper food? I'm beginning to feel hungry.'

Storm laughed delightedly. 'Trust a man to think of his stomach!' She took the tray away and sat on the bed beside him. 'You're looking better already.'

Putting his good arm round her, Luke drew her to him and kissed her. 'Where *did* you get that tent?' he wanted to know.

'Hush, it's one of Juliana's nightdresses. It's rather Victorian, isn't it?'

'I like it. It makes you look demure and virginal—and convinces me that I'm definitely getting better.'

She laughed, but as she looked at him the laughter died. 'Oh, Luke, I was so worried about you. I thought you were going to die.'

'Crazy idiot! Do you think I'd let myself die when I'd just found you?' He gave her a hug. 'You can't get rid of me that easily.'

'I don't want to get rid of you. I want to be with you always. I love you so much.' She kissed him in a sudden fierce burst of passion, then drew back laughing shakily. 'I'm sorry, I forgot that you're still weak.'

'I can take it.' He stroked her hair gently. 'I'm glad you didn't cut your hair.'

'Oh, I couldn't have done that—it's part of my stage image.'

'I suppose all your fans are crying out for you to go on another tour, or to make a new album?'

Storm nodded. 'Wayne has got lots of things lined

up for me.' She laughed happily. 'It's going to be so wonderful! Even with a manager and my dresser and everyone else you need on tour, it often seems lonely. But with you there it will be fun, we'll be able to share all the places, explore them together.'

Her face had lit in animation and she was so enthusiastic about her view of the future that she didn't see the shadow that came into Luke's eyes. But he didn't say anything, for the moment he was content to hold her and let her chatter happily on. Later, he thought, his weakened body already tiring. Later, we'll sort it out. And he fell asleep again.

The next day there was good news: the rebels had been defeated and the government troops had taken control again. 'There are still some groups of rebels who have taken to the forests and hills to be rounded up,' Dr Van Hage told them. 'But soon everything will be back to normal again.'

'Good. We'll be able to get the dam finished,' Luke commented. 'When the people have electrical power they can start getting into the twentieth century before it becomes the twenty-first.'

'It will be a great step forward,' the doctor agreed. 'It means we'll be able to have an operating theatre here on Taruna instead of having to fly the urgent cases to another island.'

On the strength of the good news, the doctor decided to drive into Bura in his old car to collect some medical supplies he needed and to make further enquiries about the men from the dam site and their families. When he came back a few hours later he had even better news. 'All your people from the dam are safe. They got through to Bura without any great trouble. And they are in touch with your brother, Storm. It seems he's been in Jakarta pushing the government to act quickly, almost since the rebellion started. Now that it's over he's going to fly here on the first available plane. Probably tomorrow.'

'Why, that's wonderful! There'll be so much to tell him. Won't he be amazed when he hears what happened to us?'

Luke smiled back at her, but there was a pinched look about his mouth and tiny beads of sweat on his forehead. Dr Van Hage glanced at him, then turned to Storm. 'As it's safe now, why don't you go for a swim in the sea? I will send a boy with you just in case, but I'm sure you will be perfectly all right.'

The idea was irresistible, and soon Storm was swimming happily in a borrowed costume of Juliana's that covered her so adequately she felt like an old-fashioned bathing belle of the twenties. But the sea felt wonderful and she went back to the house feeling completely refreshed and invigorated.

She found Luke dressed and shaved and sitting in a wicker chair in the garden.

'Hey, this is great!' she smiled. 'You look like a new man without your beard—or rather like the man you were.'

He turned to look at her, so radiantly alive and lovely, and for a second his eyes filled with pain, but then his face hardened. 'I am still the same man,' he said, almost a curt note in his voice. 'A man who has a business to run and goes around the world to get and carry out engineering projects.'

Storm frowned in perplexity. 'Why, yes, but . . .'

'No buts,' Luke said firmly. 'The way you've been

talking you expected me to just give up my business and follow you around like one of your pieces of luggage.'

'But it wouldn't be like that,' Storm said urgently. 'Sure, I'd have to work, but we'd be together.'

He gave her a harsh look. 'I've never been any woman's toy-boy, Storm, and I'm not going to start now.'

Her face flushing, Storm answered, 'I'm not asking you to be.' She hesitated as if waiting for him to speak, then said, 'You said you loved me. I thought—I thought we could get married. I thought that was what you wanted.'

'A legalised toy-boy, then,' Luke said brutally. 'No way. I'm not going to be kept by a woman.'

She gazed at him in angry uncertainty. 'Are you asking me to give up my career, is that it?' He didn't answer and she said pleadingly, 'I'm at the peak now. My records are in the top ten both in Europe and America. And I earn a lot of money, Luke, more than enough for us both. It would be—stupid to give it up now. Surely you can see that?'

'Money doesn't come into it,' he said shortly. 'And neither does marriage. I'm not changing my whole way of life just because we had sex a few times. I haven't done it for any other woman and I'm certainly not going to do it for you, pop star or not.'

It was said coarsely, and Storm shrank back from him as if he'd hit her. Her trembling hands balled into tight fists and she said unbelievingly, 'But you said you loved me.'

'Oh sure, I always tell women what they want to hear. It keeps them happy for as long as you want to use them.'

She stared at him, unable to believe what she was hearing, unable to take in this change in him. 'You—you can't mean that! Didn't it mean *anything* to you?'

His eyes ran over her body, undressing her as he went, making Storm shrivel with embarrassment and feel cheap and dirty. 'You're not a bad lay,' he conceded. 'I've known worse—and better.'

'Oh, God! How—how could you? Why are you being like this?'

'Because you were getting stupid ideas about me running round after you. No woman's worth that. When I meet a woman I want to keep then *she'll* be the one to follow *me*. And if I want to marry her I'll do the asking.' A bead of sweat trickled down his forehead and he lifted a tightly closed fist to knuckle it away. 'I've asked the doctor to lend you his car and a driver to take you to Bura. It will be safe enough now and Jerry will meet you tomorrow and make sure you get on a plane to England safely.'

'You're—you're sending me away?' whispered Storm.

'I'm sending you back where you belong. Get it into your head, Storm, it was just a pleasant interlude when neither of us had anything better to do. We got along because we had to, out there in the forest. But we're so different that being together would never work for us.'

'We could try.' She caught hold of his hand urgently, pleading so desperately that she didn't notice how hot it was. 'I'd do anything to be near you. If you really want, I'll even . . .'

'But I don't want,' Luke broke in caustically. 'Can't you get that into your head? There's no way I want you permanently around. Now that I'm well again I shall be going straight back to get the dam completed. So why don't you go and say goodbye to the Van Hages and go? The car's waiting.'

'You're getting rid of me—just like that?'

He shrugged. 'As I said, you were pretty good; maybe I'll look you up next time I'm in England.'

Boiling rage filled her heart and in that moment Storm hated him enough to kill him. 'Don't bother!' she hit out. 'I wish . . .' Her voice broke. 'I wish I'd left you to die in the forest!' Then she turned and ran stumblingly into the house.

CHAPTER EIGHT

THE SUN was shining but there was a hint of winter in the autumn air on the November day when Storm flew into London's Heathrow Airport at the end of her tour of the United States. Only Wayne Forrester and her dresser were with her, and they had deliberately kept her arrival quiet, but even so there were a couple of reporters and a photographer waiting to interview her.

'What are your plans now that your tour is over?' one of them wanted to know.

'I'm here to take part in the Royal Command Performance,' Storm answered with the professional smile that didn't reach her eyes. 'Then I have a new niece to meet and I shall be taking a holiday until after Christmas.'

They threw more questions at her which she answered goodnaturedly until one said, 'How about marriage plans, Miss Shelley? We've heard rumours that you and Mr Forrester here might be engaged?'

'There is absolutely no truth in the rumour,' Storm said coldly. 'I do *not* intend to marry.'

'Thanks, fellas, but I think that will have to be enough for now,' Wayne cut in smoothly before they could ask anything else. 'Storm has to get to London.'

Her recording company had sent a Rolls to meet her, and when they were in it, her dresser sitting in front with the chauffeur, Wayne raised the electric window between the seats so that they could be private and said, 'Did you have to deny there was anything between us quite so emphatically?'

'There isn't.'

'There could have been—before you went to visit your brother that time. You've changed a lot since then. Why won't you tell me what happened to you out there?'

'Nothing happened,' shrugged Storm.

He gave her an exasperated look. 'I wish I'd never let you go there.'

'You may be my manager, Wayne, but you're not my keeper. I'm happy to work with you, but my private life is my own.'

'You've hardly had time for any private life, the pace you've been working these last few months,' he reminded her. 'There's hardly been a day when you haven't been rehearsing or trying to write new songs.'

'Not with much success.'

'A couple you've done are good—a bit too sad, though. Why don't you try something livelier and more cheerful? Or don't you feel that way?'

'I feel fine,' she lied. 'And I'm looking forward to being a godmother to my brand new niece.'

'The christening's tomorrow, isn't it?'

'Yes. Jerry and Anne are staying with Anne's parents in Bedfordshire until they can find a house of their own. I'm going down there for the day.'

'Don't forget the first rehearsals for the Royal Command are in the morning of the day after. Have you decided what songs you want to sing?'

'Yes, I think so. They only want two, don't they?'

'Better have an encore ready,' said Wayne. 'You're said to be a favourite singer of the younger Royals.'

'All right, I'll think about it.'

Storm fell silent, looking out of the window as they sped along the motorway and remembering the last time she had arrived back in England after that disastrous trip to Taruna. She had been so hurt and bewildered by Luke's behaviour, and it had been hard to come to terms with the fact that she had fallen for a man who could be so hard and cruel. But she had been completely deceived by him until he had taken fright at her mention of marriage and shown her his true character. She was well out of it, she knew, but it had still been hard to take. Her panacea had been to throw herself into her work, cramming her diary with engagements and taking on such a punishing schedule that there had been no time to think about anything else. It hadn't done her health any good and the nightmares had come back. Only they were different now. Now she dreamt that she was lying on the oozing mud of the swamp trying to save Luke—but he lifted his hand, bringing it deliberately down on to her head and pushing her under so that she could feel the mud entering her mouth, her nostrils, her eyes. Usually then she woke up screaming and sat staring into the darkness, remembering.

Storm used a hire-car to drive out to Bedfordshire the next morning. The record company's limousine was still at her disposal, but she wanted to play down the pop star image. Today the baby was to be the star attraction, and she was determined to stay in the background as much as she could. She hadn't seen either Anne or Jerry since she had left Taruna and hadn't written to them because she hadn't wanted a letter back that might have contained news of Luke. She didn't want to know about Luke. She tried to shut him out of her mind completely. It was only in the night that she couldn't shut him out, that he crept into her dreams and her nightmares.

Anne's parents, Mr and Mrs Hobday, lived in a Georgian house in a pretty village only about a mile from the motorway. The sun was shining and the trees at the sides of the road were such a glorious blaze of autumn colours that they caught at the heart. But Storm had no eyes for beauty any more. They were trees and that was it.

Jerry came out to meet her as she pulled up in the driveway, and gave her a hug. 'Hello, little sister. Good to see you.'

'And you. How are Anne and the baby? I brought one or two things back from America for them.' And she indicated a big box full of wrapped parcels on the back seat.

'Aren't any of them for me? I'm really having my nose put out of joint,' Jerry complained, but he laughed happily as he said it and willingly carried the box indoors. Fatherhood suited him, Storm decided, he looked relaxed and contented. The dam built, his child born safely, and with a settled job in England now, according to the letter he'd sent her telling of the baby's birth and asking her to be its godmother.

She greeted Anne and her parents, and duly admired her little niece who was asleep in a lace-hung crib. 'What are you going to call her?' she asked. 'Jerry didn't say in his letter.'

'Lucy Anne.'

'Pretty.' Storm raised her eyes to look at her sister-in-law. 'You're looking very well. I take it everything went well?'

'Thanks to you. That rest in the nursing home in Darwin was exactly what I needed. I'm only sorry that you got mixed up in all that trouble on Taruna after I left.' Anne looked at Storm curiously. 'Jerry said you didn't say much about it, but it must have been quite worrying for you at the time. Especially when Luke . . .'

'It wasn't worrying so much as annoying,' Storm cut in quickly. 'I just couldn't wait to get back to civilisation!' She smiled and took Anne's hand. 'Come on, aren't you going to open the baby's presents?'

This proved a more than adequate distraction, Anne soon excitedly exclaiming in pleasure at all the baby clothes and toys that Storm had brought for her niece. There were presents for Jerry and Anne too, so that they wouldn't feel left out, but they had obviously become doting parents already and had completely forgotten themselves in their shared love for the child.

The christening ceremony, which was to be held in the local church where Anne and Jerry had been married, was to take place at three o'clock. They had a light lunch first and then Anne took the baby upstairs to feed it and get it and herself ready. While she was upstairs the guests started to arrive. They were mostly relations and old girlfriends of Anne's, with just a few friends of Jerry's that Storm knew and could talk to.

At twenty to three Jerry started to get impatient to leave, so Storm ran upstairs to get her coat, afterwards following Anne down again. But at the bottom of the stairs Anne exclaimed, 'Oh, my handbag! I've left it upstairs.'

'Can I get it for you?'

'Er—no, I'd better go. I want to get a couple of hankies as well in case Lucy dribbles. Here, take her for me, will you, Storm? I won't be a minute.'

'Oh, but . . .'

Anne laughed. 'Don't be afraid. You'll have to hold her during the ceremony, anyway.'

Having no experience whatsoever of babies, Storm was terrified lest she should drop it or do it some harm, but she took the baby and held it carefully in her arms. It was so minute and small, much too tiny for the long lace christening robe and the beautiful shawl in which it was wrapped. It lay asleep, long lashes fluttering on milk-white cheeks, tiny little bubbles of air on perfect little rosebud lips. Her hands were mostly curled into fists, but every now and again she opened them to reveal fingers that were so delicate and yet so perfect. And she smelt so beautiful, of warmth and milk and newness.

Storm stood in the hall, holding the child and concentrating entirely on it, her eyes wide and tender with wonder as she realised for the first time how a baby could catch at your heart and hold it fast. The doorbell rang again and someone went to open it, but she was too intent on her niece to look up. But then a feeling of sharp tension penetrated her senses and she lifted her head to see Luke standing in the hallway. The blood drained from her face as she stood in frozen numbness, too stunned to even think.

Luke gazed back at her for a long moment, a look almost of consternation in his eyes. His jaw hardened and he took a couple of steps towards her, but Jerry came out of the drawing-room, walking quickly, his hand outstretched. 'Luke! Great to see you. I was beginning to be afraid you weren't going to make it.'

Luke murmured something about a traffic hold-up on the motorway, his eyes still on Storm.

Jerry followed his gaze and thought he was looking at the baby. 'Come and meet your goddaughter,' he invited.

Storm stiffened, feeling trapped, her hands involuntarily tightening so that the baby stirred and gave a tiny wail of protest.

Pleased that his daughter was awake, Jerry gave her his finger to hold. 'Isn't she beautiful? Anne's mother thinks she looks exactly like Anne at that age.'

Luke glanced at the baby, but then his eyes went back to Storm, his gaze raking over her. 'Hello, Storm.'

She didn't like that look, it was almost as if he were trying to see into her soul. Her chin came up and she said to Jerry, 'Isn't it time we were leaving? If you'll take her I'll go and get my bag.'

'Oh. Well. Er—Anne, are you ready?'

His call brought Anne hurrying down, and Storm was able to slip away as she took the baby and greeted Luke. If she hadn't been a godparent Storm would have left the house and gone back to London there and then, and to hell with what everybody thought.

She might have done it anyway if it hadn't been for those few moments when she had held the tiny child and fallen in love with her niece. Now she wanted to be part of Lucy's life, and if she wanted that she could hardly walk out on her right at the beginning.

On the walk to the church she took good care to keep out of Luke's way, staying close beside one of Jerry's old friends, which flattered the man's ego considerably but didn't please his wife at all. But at the church she had no choice but to be close to Luke as they stood around the font. He took his place beside her, and gave her a sardonic look when she immediately took a side step farther away. The ceremony wasn't very long, but for Storm it was deeply moving. As she watched the age-old ceremony, the sun shafting through the stained glass window to cover them in rich gold and blues and reds, she too felt timeless, and as if her life might perhaps have some purpose after all. When it was time for her to hold the child and give its name, she felt for a moment that she didn't want to give it back, and silly tears pricked at her eyes. She turned away and found Luke watching her—and suddenly everything was back to normal again, her heart filled with hate and bitterness. Almost she laughed aloud and thought, God, some normality!

The solemnity over, there was a lot of laughter on the walk back to the house and during the party following it. Mrs Hobday and Anne had laid on a very good buffet. There was plenty of wine, a beautifully decorated christening cake and champagne to drink when they cut it, and Luke proposed a toast to baby Lucy. He did it humorously and well, bringing a

flush of pleasure to Anne's cheeks and making Jerry
smile with pride. But Luke hadn't finished. Turning
to face Storm across the room, he said in the deep
masculine voice that she remembered so well, 'And I
must of course include my fellow godparent with my
good wishes. I'm quite sure that when Lucy gets to be
a teenager Storm will be far more popular than I will.
But if Lucy has even a half of her aunt's courage and
kindness, of her beauty and talent, then she'll be a
very fortunate child indeed.' He paused, his grey eyes
holding Storm's as there was a murmur of agreement
through the room, then smiled and raised his glass.
'Ladies and gentlemen, I give you the toast of good
health, long life and happiness to Lucy Anne Shelley.'

Everyone drank, and talk became general again as
Anne's mother passed round pieces of cake. Storm
stood in a corner, trying to make herself as
unobtrusive as possible and wondering why the hell
Luke had described her as he had. Because she'd
saved his life? But whatever it was, that had been a
damn fool thing to say. Swallowing down the
champagne, she refused a piece of cake and edged her
way towards the door, intending to slip quietly away.
She could always phone when she got to London
to apologise, make some excuse or other for not
staying.

Someone she had never met before detained her,
asking for an autograph. She scribbled it hastily and
managed to move away and out of the room. The
coats had all been put in a small room opening off the
back of the hall that Anne's father used as a study.
With a sigh of relief Storm put on her fur jacket and
turned to leave just as Luke followed her, shutting the

door firmly behind him.

'Leaving already?'

Ignoring him, she strode towards the door, but he reached out and caught her arm.

'I spoke to you.' She didn't answer, just glared at him angrily, until his lip curled scornfully. 'I can't stand women who sulk.'

She gave him a look of pure venom. 'I'm not sulking. You're just not worth wasting my breath on.'

His grip tightened for a moment, but he gave a small sigh. 'I guess I deserved that. Storm, I have to talk to you. There was a . . .'

'Well, I don't want to talk to you.' She tried to shake him off, but he held her fast. 'Damn you, let go of me!'

'Not until you've heard what I've got to say. Let's take a walk round the garden.'

'No. I'm leaving.'

'Running away, you mean. If I still have that much effect on you maybe it means that you're still in love with me.'

She laughed scornfully, tilting her head back, her golden hair tumbling like threads of fine silk on her black jacket. 'Yes, you have an effect on me—you just make me remember how much I hate you.'

'Really?' Luke moved nearer, his eyes purposeful. 'Somehow I don't believe that.'

'If you touch me I'll scream the place down!'

She said it in a voice so low and fierce that he stopped short. 'I really believe you would.' His lips curled in an almost painful smile. 'You always did have a damn loud scream!' But instead of letting her go his grasp tightened on her arm. 'All right, so we'll

go outside.' And pulling her after him, he opened the
french doors and went into the garden, walking
rapidly away from the house.

It happened so quickly that Storm had no time to
protest, Luke's hold on her arm vicelike as he
propelled her across the lawn and through a
shrubbery until they were out of sight of the house.
When he stopped she was panting and had no breath
to scream as he drew her roughly into his arms and
kissed her. Taken by surprise, she was pliant for a
moment, her lips soft and yielding under his, but then
her body grew rigid with furious resentment and she
struggled so much that he had to let her go.

'You bastard!' she shrieked at him, rubbing her
hand across her mouth in revulsion. 'I could kill
you!'

'Why? Because you still feel something for me, isn't
that why? Listen, Storm,' he took hold of her
shoulders, his voice urgent, 'when I told you I loved
you back in Taruna it was the truth. But I had to send
you away because . . .' He broke off as she began to hit
out at him. 'Keep still, you wildcat, and listen!'
Catching hold of her wrists, he pulled them behind
her back, holding her firmly.

Storm glared at him, her hair a dishevelled halo
around her head. 'You pig! I'm not going to listen to
anything you . . .'

'Yes, you are.' Luke jerked her into silence. 'I had to
send you away from Taruna—I had no choice. But I
lied when I said it hadn't meant anything. You were
the most wonderful thing that ever happened to me,
and I loved you so much. It nearly broke my heart to
send you away. But I owed you so much that I had to

do it. I couldn't take the risk. I had no right to push that kind of responsibility on to you.'

'What risk? What are you talking about?' Despite her anger, Storm's eyes were fixed on his face.

'That last day, I felt ill again. And when Dr Van Hage examined it he found that my arm was worse. He told me that he thought it quite probable it would have to come off.'

Storm stared at him in stunned shock. 'You would lose your arm?'

'Yes.'

She broke free of his grip suddenly and caught hold of his left arm, gave a gasp of relief when she felt strong human muscle.

'I wouldn't let them do it,' he told her. 'I made them fly me to a specialist hospital in Australia where they tried everything, and eventually it began to heal. It was touch and go for quite a while, but I was determined to keep it.' He smiled down at her. 'A man needs two arms when he tells a girl how much he loves her.' And he put both his arms round her to demonstrate.

Storm took a deep breath, still hardly able to grasp what he was telling her. She looked up into his face, at his eyes smiling tenderly down at her—and was filled with a violent rage. Pushing him away, she snapped out, 'How dare you? How *dare* you make that kind of decision for me? You should have told me.'

'No.' Luke shook his head vehemently. 'If I'd told you, you would have stayed, and it would have made it that much harder to make you leave me if I'd lost my arm.'

'I wouldn't have left you,' Storm broke in

passionately. 'It wouldn't have made any difference to me.'

'But it *would* to me. Storm, you'd already said that you wanted to go on with your career and for me to abandon mine. To be kept by you when I was in one piece would have been bad enough, but to be a cripple . . .' His jaw hardened. 'I didn't intend to be a charity case for the rest of my life. No way.'

'Love isn't charity.'

'Maybe it wouldn't have been for you—not at first, at any rate. But it certainly would have looked that way to the rest of the world. And eventually you would have come to think that way too, and you would have lost any respect you ever had for me. I wasn't about to let it happen, Storm. The last thing I ever wanted to see in your eyes was pity.'

'I loved you. I loved you for—for better or worse. It wouldn't have mattered.'

'It would have mattered to me.' Reaching out, Luke took hold of her by the arms. 'Storm, try and see it from my point of view. I would have lost my independence, my pride, my ambition, and eventually my masculinity. I would have made your life hell and mine as well. So it had to be that way. Please try and accept that,' he pleaded urgently.

Storm stood silent for a moment, then raised her head, her beautiful blue eyes colder than the winter sky. 'I don't have any choice, do I? All right, so why bother to tell me all this?'

'I hadn't intended to,' Luke admitted slowly. 'I'd been following what you were doing through a press agency. I was afraid you might marry your manager, but they just sent me lists of recording sessions, appearances, charity shows and tours. By the time I was well enough to come back to England it seemed as if you were firmly established back in your career. That even if I went to you and told you why I'd made you leave me, it wouldn't have made any difference, you would still have wanted me to give up my business and follow you.'

'You keep saying "follow me",' Storm broke in, 'but you could quite easily have made my career your business instead. You could have taken over from Wayne as my manager. You could have *joined* me and we could have shared . . .' She bit her lip and looked away. 'But that's in the past—unless you've changed your mind.'

'No. I'm no Svengali to your Trilby.' He shook his head, and Storm turned and walked away so that he wouldn't see the tearing disappointment in her eyes. 'That hasn't changed—but you've changed.' Coming up behind her, he made her turn round to face him. 'I knew you were going to be here today, but I'd made up my mind not to tell you anything—not to let you see that I still loved you.' He paused, his voice changing. 'But when I walked into the hall and saw you holding that child—saw the love and tenderness on your face as you looked at it . . .' His voice grew husky and he had to clear his throat. 'Well, then I knew that you were ready for marriage. For a real marriage with a settled home and babies like Lucy. So that's why I'm telling you all this. Because I love you and I want you to marry me, my darling love.'

'And to give up my career?' she said.

'Yes, that too. We don't need it, Storm,' he urged. 'All we need is each other.'

'That's what I thought—until you made me leave
you behind in Taruna.' Pulling herself free of his
hold, she cried out passionately, 'If you'd asked me
then, told me how much it meant to you, I would have
gladly given up my career. I would have done
anything for you. And I would have gone on loving
you even if you'd lost both your arms and both your
legs and your—your . . .'

Luke gave a low laugh. 'Spare me what's left—I've a
feeling I'm going to need it!' he grinned.

But Storm shook her head, her eyes scornful, and
went on as if he hadn't spoken. 'But you didn't love
me enough to even give me a chance to do anything
for you. You sent me away as if I meant nothing to
you. The only time you showed any—kindness for me
was when you made me hate you.'

She went to walk past him back to the house, but
Luke caught her wrist. 'I had to let you go,' he said
fiercely. 'I owed you my life.'

Her face cold and contemptuous, Storm said, 'Your
life is nothing to me.' And shaking off his arm, she
kept on walking.

The rehearsals for the Command Performance were
organised chaos, with everyone trying to rehearse as
much as possible in as short a time as possible, the
acts timed to a minute and carefully worked out to
build to a big climax. Storm was one of the easy ones
because she didn't have to have any costumes fitted,
she knew her songs and exactly how she wanted them
played. Just before she left the rehearsal one of the
organisers came up and asked if she wanted any
tickets. After a moment she bought three in the front

row of the dress circle and sent them off to Jerry, thinking that he and Anne and one of her parents might like to come, leaving the other parent at home to babysit.

Apart from work, Storm was very withdrawn, sitting alone in her flat brooding over how her life might have been if only Luke had loved her enough to let her care instead of insisting on being the one to make all the sacrifices. Wayne first of all tried to find out what had happened, but wasn't surprised when she didn't tell him; he had got used to having lost her confidence in the last few months. So he tried to talk about work, asking her to discuss the terms of her new recording contract, to start booking appearances for the new year and to decide which of two tours she was going to do first.

'The Australian tour might be the best,' he suggested. 'You could do it in their winter when people are more likely to go to the theatre. And that would tie in with the new album the recording company want you to make.'

Storm thought of Luke lying in hospital in Australia, fighting to save his arm in lonely pride. 'I don't want to go to Australia,' she said definitely.

'Well, all right, we'll do the European tour instead.'

'I don't want to go to Europe either!'

Wayne looked at her exasperatedly. 'What is it with you, Storm? One minute you're asking me to get you as much work as possible, and now you don't want to do it.'

'I'm sorry.' She put her hands up to her head. 'I just can't decide at the moment. But I'll think about it, I promise.'

Wayne stood up, hesitated, then said harshly, 'You're in love with someone else; I've known that ever since you got back from Indonesia. And I know that it hasn't worked out for you. But my offer still stands, Storm. I still want to marry you.' Taking her hand, he held it and said persuasively, 'Why not, Storm? We make a great partnership, don't we?'

'Svengali and Trilby,' murmured Storm, remembering. 'I'm sorry, Wayne.' She looked at him unhappily and said in a sudden burst of candour, 'I think it would be best if you looked for a new job. I'm not giving you the sack or anything—it's just that I don't know if I want to go on singing any more.'

'But that's crazy! You're at the top now.'

'Yes, but I'm different. My values are different. I've got enough money to last me for the rest of my life. And I don't want fame any more. There isn't any fun and excitement left, Wayne. Surely you've seen that for yourself? There's nothing to look forward to now, so I think it might be best if I get out before—before it all gets on top of me again.'

'You're not thinking straight,' Wayne said sharply. 'Look—OK, maybe I've been pushing you a bit too hard. We'll leave deciding on any of these contracts until after the Command Performance. Maybe you'll be less tense then.'

So it was left in the air, but even backstage on the night of the performance Storm felt no excitement. She had to share a dressing-room with three other women, one of them a well-known comedienne turned chat-show host, who kept opening the door and shouting for her manager to find out exactly what time she was on, to phone her home, to make sure her guests had arrived, to see if there were any good-luck telegrams for her, until the poor man was rushed off his feet.

When she impatiently went out of the room to find him when he didn't come the minute she called, the other two women immediately started talking about her. 'Poor devil,' one remarked. 'I'm surprised he doesn't find himself another job—nothing could be worse than her.'

'He can't,' the other replied. 'He isn't her manager, he's her husband. He married her for her money and she's making him pay for it.'

Storm listened but didn't join in. Would people have thought of Luke like that, she wondered, if he'd married her and become her manager? She changed into her dress: long, white and strapless, the skirt slit up to her knees at the front, and covered in sequins that would catch all the spotlights that would be on her. With it there was a matching loose jacket that she hadn't intended to wear, but now she put it on and looked at herself in the full-length mirror. Yes, she would keep the jacket. She should really have had a necklace, but that had disappeared in the swamp and she hadn't bothered to replace it. Somehow jewellery didn't seem at all important any more. What was the point in showing off your neck if the one man in the world you wanted wasn't there to see it?

But in that she was wrong. One of the messenger boys came to the dressing-room with some telegrams, several baskets and bouquets of flowers, and a small parcel for her. Storm glanced at the cards with the flowers, but the parcel intrigued her and she opened it before the telegrams. It contained a velvet jeweller's box embossed with a famous name, and inside was a gold pendant necklace, the pendant an exact replica of the guitar that she'd had on Taruna. Slowly Storm took the pendant from the case, her lips curving a little as she remembered Luke saying that he knew he'd fallen in love with her when he saw her bash the guitar over the rebel's head. And how it had saved his life in the swamp. She had told him that no other guitar could ever take its place—but as she stroked this golden miniature she began to wonder.

There was a card inside the box. It read simply, 'I'll never stop loving you. I'll be in the theatre tonight. Come to me, my darling.'

The words plucked at her memory, reminding her of an old song. Getting quickly to her feet, she ran out of the dressing-room to find one of the stage managers, speaking to him urgently. He threw up his arms at her request but went to do as she asked, coming back after the next act to say, 'It's all right, they've got the music and they'll do it, but you'll have to do the lead in.'

'Thank you, oh, thank you!' Storm surprised the man by giving him an impulsive hug. 'Now if you could do one thing more for me. I bought tickets for some seats in the dress circle. If you could just point out to me where they are . . .'

Storm stood waiting in the wings, filled with excitement, but this was no stage fright, it was a very different, very heady exhilaration that ran through her veins. The act before hers came off and the compère went on to announce her. She walked on to the huge stage to a wave of applause and anticipation, the sea of faces just a sea of faces, no longer hungry for her soul. She curtsied to the Royal Box and stood, a slim white and gold figure against the deep red of the curtains, the pendant around her neck.

She sang two numbers to a great thunder of applause and appreciation which didn't stop until she held up her hand. 'Thank you for so much, ladies and gentlemen.' She paused, then added on a firm note of happiness, 'I should like to take this opportunity of saying goodbye to you and all my fans who have been so very kind to me in the past. This is the last professional appearance I shall ever make, and I should like to sing this very last song to the very special person that I'm going to spend the rest of my life with.'

After a murmur of concerned amazement a hush fell over the audience. Storm's eyes lifted above the stalls to the seats in the circle that she had had pointed out to her. It was difficult to see through the spotlights, but she knew Luke was out there, listening. The music started and she began to sing. 'I'll never stop loving you, whatever else I may do.'

The orchestra joined in softly, then rising as she sang on. 'My love for you will last till time itself is through.'

The last note faded as the music slowly died. Storm smiled and waved, acknowledged the tumultuous ovation, then turned and walked away from the glare of the lights into her future with the man she loved.

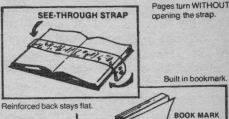

Harlequin American Romance

Romances that go one step farther...
American Romance

Realistic stories involving people you can relate to and
care about.

Compelling relationships between the mature men and
women of today's world.

Romances that capture the core of genuine emotions
between a man and a woman.

Join us each month for four new titles wherever paperback
books are sold.
Enter the world of American Romance.

Harlequin Superromance

Here are the longer, more involving stories you have been waiting for... Superromance.

Modern, believable novels of love, full of the complex joys and heartaches of real people.

Intriguing conflicts based on today's constantly changing life-styles.

Four new titles every month.
Available wherever paperbacks are sold.

SUPER-1
